Duncaster

D1175170

STYGO

STYGO

LAURA HENDRIE

MACMURRAY & BECK

ASPEN

1994

F
Hen

Printed and bound in the United States of America
Library of Congress Catalog Card Number: 93-080394

Publisher's Cataloging in Publication
(Prepared by Quality Books Inc.)

Hendrie, Laura.
    Stygo / by Laura Hendrie.
    p. cm.
    ISBN 1-878448-59-5

    I. Title.

PS3558.H453S8 1994   813'.54
                                                      QBI93-22177

"Arroyo" appeared in *The Missouri Review.*

MacMurray & Beck Fiction: General Editor, Greg Michalson

*Book design and illustrations by Paulette Livers Lambert. The
illustrations for this book were executed on scratchboard. The text
was set in Bembo, with heads in Copperplate Gothic, by Argent
Associates of Boulder, Colorado.*

8181

This book is for Mark
—most loving, most beloved—

CONTENTS

My deep gratitude to those who supported and inspired my efforts to complete this book, including Don Hendrie Jr., Andre Dubus, Alan Wier, Bob and Catfish, Claudia Johnson, Tom Rabbit, Pierre Delattre, Richard Giles, Dunya Bean, Suzanne Tate, Kelly Wolpert, my sister Ellen and my mother, Nip.

As we rush, as we rush in the train,
The trees and the houses go wheeling back,
But the starry heavens above the plain
Come flying on our track.

—James Thomson
1834–1882

O N E

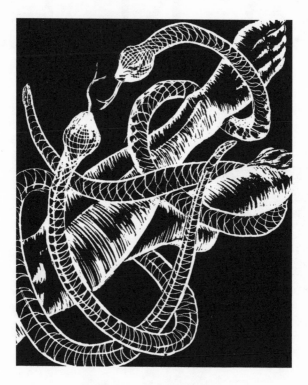

STYGO
AT NIGHT

That spring, everybody in Stygo said you had to watch where you stepped. Jake Loper had found a four-footer in the middle of Main Street, stretched out like it owned the place, with a head big around as a man's fist. He pinned it with John Wackett's crutch while Harley Barrows ran for the meat cleaver. Since the Red Spot Sugar Beet bosses insisted that they had solved the rattlesnake problem by dynamiting the nest east of town, everybody in town met at Frank's bar that night to have a look at the one Jake killed. That happened on a Wednesday, the only Wednesday Lizzy could recall where the Rockeroy stayed wild until last call.

Usually people waited until Friday to celebrate. Some Fridays Frank lured in a band from Springer, but even if he didn't, people came. There wasn't much else around except the carnival in Funtown, and you couldn't get there if you didn't own wheels. Now and then, somebody with a grudge and too much booze got out of control—words, tears, fist-fights and such. But on the whole people got along, and it seemed to Lizzy that, with the exception of the rattler scare, the first year of her marriage to Jake Loper was passing just as smoothly as every other year of her life had.

■

Jake had gotten an air cooler for summers, but by June the sound of it in their trailer unnerved her, made her feel as if what she was hearing was not the cooling system at all but the sound of the heat building up outside. Sometimes when she fell asleep, she dreamed that it was already August and the heat outside was beginning to melt the aluminum hinges of the air vents closed. On those days it was better to go sit next to the fan in the front room at the Rockeroy until everybody who worked at the refinery got back to town. Usually, she wore her everyday clothes to the bar and carried what she wanted to wear that night in a box to keep it from getting dusty. On this Friday, she carried the new turquoise blouse Jake had bought her on his last trip to Mason City.

The Rockeroy had at one time been called the Grazier—which was still visible through the whitewash above the door—but that was before the anthrax hit, and before the Red Spot Sugar Beet Company moved in to revive the town. Frank had renamed it the Rockeroy in honor of the rocker plates that moved the beets into the slicers, only the paint was no good over mudbrick, and every summer the name peeled and had to be repainted. When Lizzy stepped up on the porch, the dried red and blue chips crunched under her thongs.

No one was there yet except Tom Go, who was crouched over the pinball machine behind the door, making it ding. Tom Go had fire-red hair and skin the color of watery milk. He was at the stage of life where he rarely smiled at women, where he kept his FEED cap pulled so low over his eyes that when he played pinball he had to lean backwards to see his score. He'd been nicknamed Go because of his decision to move to Alaska, a dream he'd taken on with such deadly conviction that he had a second-hand Arctic parka rotting in the back of his closet at home. People who knew about it called it Tom Go's secret weapon. When Lizzy opened the door, he rammed another dime into the machine, spread his legs, and shot.

Lizzy told him to bring her a Red River and went to the ladies' room. The bathroom mirror rattled from his thrusts against the pinball machine on the other side of the ply-wood. "Tom?" she called, checking over her shoulder to see how the new shirt looked from the back. And then louder, "Are you working here or not, Tom Go?" When she came out, he threw himself away from his game and stormed off into the kitchen. Lizzy took a seat at the counter, removed her compact, and opened it to check her makeup.

Moving the mirror to one side, she spotted Kwami behind her in the booth by the window, sucking on a candy. Because of a fall she'd taken off the Milk River bridge, Kwami's mind had become unfixed. Most people were of the opinion that her father, Billy Quail, who worked for Frank, should send her over to Mama Jewell's, where they looked after people like that, but Kwami was always in the bar, sitting blank as a bug, at least until Happy Hour came, when Billy would come out of the kitchen and send her downstairs to her room. Tom Go came back holding a bag of ice and a scoop. Lizzy closed the compact and gave him her smile.

"Go easy on the sweet stuff, please. Last time you made it too thick. How's Alaska going?"

Tom's cheeks turned pink. He shoved a glass onto the counter, slopped in ice, syrup and soda, stuck in a cherry, and pushed the drink across the counter.

"Just put it on our tab." Lizzy shooed away a fly, dropped her purse on the stool next to her, and pulled the glass closer. Without using her hands, she took the straw in her mouth. When she looked up, Tom turned pink all the way out to the ends of his ears. He rammed his hands in his back pockets, and slunk back to his game.

Lizzy closed her eyes and sucked. There was nothing better than a Friday afternoon at the Rockeroy with the fan and a Red River to keep you cool. Another dime shot into the pinball machine and the rocket balls rattled down in their slots.

Jake had been the one to introduce her to Red Rivers. He had worked Tom Go's job back then, and Lizzy had come in every afternoon for a Red River because of him. Jake had been almost as shy of her as Tom was—but that was the problem with growing up pretty in a small town, everybody was scared of you. In another way it was nice, Lizzy had to remind herself, because ever since the night she'd told Jake to kiss her, he had never stopped honeymooning her. In fact, nothing had really changed, except now they were married and now Jake worked at the sugar refinery instead of the Rockeroy. Now they drank Red Spot rum and Cokes together instead of Red Rivers. But they were still happy. Even when she deserved it, Jake never raised his voice. Not like Harley Barrows, who slapped his girl, Baby Annie, around for anything—being too pretty, being sober, being pregnant, anything. Frank's sister, Pearl Stiles, who waitressed the bar Friday nights, said Lizzy was the luckiest girl in town. Sometimes Pearl's face got a little ugly when she said it, especially when she drank, but that was Pearl. She'd turned down Oren Whatly, thinking Lizzy didn't have a snake's chance in heaven with Jake. Now Pearl drank too much and swore like a man and nobody asked her out unless they had no money to tip.

Lizzy looked at the new rattler skin on the wall and then at the Coors waterfall clock. Jake would be getting in line at the bank with his paycheck. She glanced over her shoulder. Kwami had disappeared almost as if she'd never been there, as if she'd vanished into air, something that was not unusual but always a relief. Lizzy took three dimes out of her purse, picked up her drink and went through the saloon doors to the back room.

The lights were still off but the jukebox in the corner gave off a pink glow. She felt her way around the pool table, put in a dime, punched 20A, and Frankie Lyman began "Looks Like Home to Me." It hit Lizzy every time. Since there was nobody to complain, she put in her other dimes and pressed 20A twice more, remembering how she'd stood on this very spot, a little drunk, humming along with Frankie into Jake's ear, how she had hooked one finger over the top of his collar so that it barely touched his neck, how he had shivered when she did and said, "Oh honey, this changes everything."

The lights came on behind the bar. Frank was at the register counting out money and Tom Go was in back of him tapping on Shirley's aquarium. Shirley was a big diamondback rattler almost as old as Tom Go. Frank had found her and ten or eleven of her brothers and sisters under Mama Jewell's porch, but Shirley was the only one who had survived. Back when Jake worked for Frank, Shirley's aquarium had been streaked cloudy with venom, but nowadays Shirley knew better than to waste her energy. She didn't react at all to Tom Go's tapping, but her dinner, a little white mouse, jumped to attention and, for lack of a better place, perched on top of her head.

Frank slapped Tom Go's hand away from the aquarium and handed him some money. "Don't go spending it all on mukluks, neither."

Tom Go turned to leave and saw Lizzy. Face on fire, he knocked his cap around so the bill was in the front, shoved his hands in his back pockets, and slammed out the swinging saloon doors. A moment later the screen door in the outer room crashed shut. Frank winced.

"Lord, but I'll be glad when he's over that stage," he said. "But then, I guess he will be, too." Frank laughed that big har-har of his, the one that always surprised you because he was such a shy, gray cow of a man. He picked his scoop out of the bar sink and waved it at the door. "Fact is, the kid's slow. Hasn't got interest in nothing but Alaska and pinball yet that I can see."

"Give him time," said Lizzy. She went over to stand at the bar. It was not hard to picture Tom Go shaking off the sugar dust from a day at the refinery, some girl beside him oohing Shirley, leaning on the bar while Frank made them drinks. "He'll come around," said Lizzy. "Except for the color of his hair, he's no different. He just tries to think he is."

It seemed a sad thing to say. Frank sighed and looked up at the clock. "Happy hour." He held out his hand and she gave him her glass. He dumped it in the sink, and they both fell silent to watch his hands fix her a Red Spot and Coke.

"Thank God I only got a month left." It was Johanna Whatly, hair fixed up like a cyclone, eight months into her fourth kid, waving at herself to cool off. She lowered herself with a grunt into a booth against the back wall. "If I were you, Liz, I'd get your first one going in summer, that way, by the time you swell up to this size," patting her belly, "the snow'll be here and you won't have to suffer the heat like I do. Every October I go, Oren, now you keep your pants buttoned until February at least so as I don't have to be swollen up for summer. But you know men. Let just one bad snowstorm keep them from getting to the bar at night for a game of pool and suddenly they haven't got a single idea in their heads of what else to do with theirselves but get another hard-on. . . . oh, now Frank," she chided. "Look at him, Lizzy. Blushing like he's never heard a woman say hard-on. Frank? Hard-on. It's just the facts of life. If you can't listen then don't. Make me something cold, okay?" She took a bag of makeup out of her purse and spread tubes and bottles out on the table. "But when I saw you cross the street, Lizzy, I told myself, Johanna, baby or no baby, heat or no heat, go let her in on the news."

Lizzy took the drink Frank had made for her and tasted it.

"The news," pressed Johanna, "of who's come back all of a sudden."

Lizzy turned around. "Who, Johanna."

"Willa Moon, that's who." Johanna unscrewed a purple tube of eyeliner. "Just like I predicted."

Lizzy sat down. "You're fooling."

She pursed her lips and leered sideways at herself in the compact's mirror, trying to get the tip of the brush into the corner of her eye. "Am not."

"Was she with anybody?"

"Nope." Frank moved out from behind the bar and crossed the room with Johanna's drink. "She came in this morning on the Greyhound and walked straight to the hotel.

Alone. Harley says she came with a suitcase and a grocery bag of booze and hasn't been seen out since. I was over at the filling station. I'd have seen her if she'd gotten back on the bus this afternoon, but she didn't. She hasn't even come back out of the hotel yet."

When Frank realized he was being stared at, he looked down at the drink in his hand, set it before Johanna and returned to the bar. The back of his neck was crimson.

"My goodness." Johanna closed her compact. "And here I thought only Lizzy would be interested in Willa Moon's return—"

"For God's sake." Frank banged a bag of ice on the floor and broke it into the sink. "What business is it of yours?"

"Why, you're absolutely right," said Johanna, sliding her drink closer. "It's none of our business. Is it, Liz honey?"

Frank rolled his eyes. He picked up the ice scoop and then angrily threw it down. "Where's the fruit that boy was supposed to cut for me. It's Friday, isn't it? So where the hell are my limes?" He threw his bar rag in the sink and went into the kitchen.

Johanna watched him leave and then opened a lipstick. "If I didn't know better," she murmured, "I'd say the oldest male virgin in town is snake-bit. Wouldn't you?" She clicked shut her lipstick, took out a cigarette and a lighter. "Got an ashtray over there, Liz? My Oren's been after me to quit, but I tell him if I have to deprive myself of cigarettes, then fair's fair, he's got to deprive himself of alcohol. That shuts up a man, believe me." She paused and then, craning up over the top of her seat to look in the next booth, she gave a sharp cry. "What are *you* doing there in the dark?" Kwami Quail ducked out of the booth and fled under the saloon doors.

Johanna shivered and reached up to turn on the light over her booth. "Gives me the creeps, the way she's always sneaking around this place when you least expect it, staring at things. I wish Oren'd do something about her. Seems to me, being sheriff, he has as much right to help Billy Quail decide what's best for her as any doctor. Oh, wait. Never mind the ashtray," she said, though Lizzy had not moved. "There's one here behind the sugar."

"So anyhow," She blew smoke out her nose the French way. "As I remember it, Willa Moon and you were friends for a while. Am I right?"

■

You whoring black rattler cat. That was what Billy Fiddle yelled the night he caught Willa Moon necking with a townie down in the culvert that ran under the railroad tracks. Billy had slapped her face in front of the boy and said her dead mother was one, too. Willa Moon had laughed; at least that's what she told Lizzy when they sneaked there the next night with wine and lemon drops. The only time you went to the culvert was after dark. In the day, to escape the heat, that's where rattlers slept.

After they finished the wine, Willa stood on tiptoes and leaned back to write on the culvert ceiling, her hair falling down her back like a black river. Lizzy remembered the rough bite of wine in the back of her throat as she crouched, giggling, with the flashlight and bottle between her knees. DO THE RATTLER CAT FUCK seemed nastier than all the other dirty words scribbled in the culvert. To this day Jake could do certain things to her in bed that reminded her of the smell of yellow chalk on wet cement. She would tell Willa that when she saw her.

Yes, they'd been friends, in spite of Lizzy's father forbidding it. Best friends for a while, at least until Lizzy started going to the Rockeroy for Red Rivers. Willa Moon thought Jake was a bore. She called him Mr. Clean. When Lizzy showed up in the culvert wearing Jake's engagement ring, Willa called her a sellout and Lizzy called Willa a tramp, and that had been that. Lizzy's father couldn't have been happier. He gave Jake a promotion in the beet sorting room. At the wedding, when he stood up to give the toast, he told everyone his daughter had finally come to her senses. Lizzy had resented it—so sure of himself, as if he'd managed Lizzy the same way he'd managed the slicers at the refinery for twenty-one years. But after the wedding, it was a relief to be on good terms with him again, to not be so angry all the time. She let him say what he wanted.

And then that older brother of Mary Angel's showed up in Stygo, that Mick Angel, with nothing to show for himself but a big dark purple car with the muffler torn off and a little dog named Dirty Pants that he kept on a string. He said he'd been everywhere and wasn't going to stay. He smelled of gasoline and tequila and he had a hungry way of staring that frightened nearly everybody but Willa. Lizzy predicted it, she told Jake she could see it coming, what with Willa's wild streak and all, but still it was a shock when Willa Moon left with him. She didn't even wave good-bye. There were rumors, but nobody could say for sure, not until the FBI showed up, asking directions to Ester Angel's place. Oren Whatly, who took them out to Funtown in his squad car, said afterwards that they were interested in Mick because a family named Winkers had been murdered over in Mason City. Lizzy thought Oren had let the power of being sheriff go to his head—that, and the fear of being a nobody to his wife—but Oren was right. A month later, Lizzy heard on the television that Mick Angel had been caught up in North Dakota and confessed. She couldn't believe it was the same Mick Angel, but there he was, right on her TV. According to the reporters, he hadn't even known the Winkers, he had just decided to follow them home one night after they left Funtown. Three kids and two adults. Willa Moon had been arrested, too, but she'd been released. Lizzy read the newspapers and watched the newscasts. There were editorials and exposés and news briefs and even talk shows devoted to understanding Mick Angel. But nothing more on Willa Moon, on who she was or where she had gone since.

The screen door out in the front room slapped and a moment later the sugar workers began filing in, pink-eyed and gray with sugar-dust, cigarettes hanging off their mouths. Hank Berard drew up beside Lizzy, nudged her hello and slapped the bar for service. Frank came out of the kitchen with a tray of limes, Pearl followed, patting her hair into place, the mouse in Shirley's cage stretched high to sniff the air, its forefeet like tiny hands on the glass, and the room filled with the first howls of Friday night.

The twins, Lee and Billy Fiddle, pressed up against the bar in a cloud of cigar smoke to shout for a round of Red Spot and Lizzy looked down at her drink, remembering the night she and Willa had gotten sick on cigars and decided to draw up a blood-sister pact. Lizzy couldn't make herself draw blood with the steak knife Willa had stolen, so they decided to touch tongues instead. The Rattler Cat Tongue-Sister Pact. They giggled so hard they couldn't stand up, and when the small, hard tips of their tongues touched, Lizzy was so surprised that she dropped the flashlight and they bumped heads in the dark. The kunk sound of skull hitting skull echoed in the culvert, and that had been funny, too.

An arm smelling of the green tar soap Frank kept in the bathrooms slid around her neck from behind.

"Now I ask you, guys. Have I got a good-looking wife here or what."

"No doubt about it," mooed Frank, holding out a drink without looking up. "You're a lucky man." Frank liked Jake. Everybody liked Jake. Jake took the drink in his fist and kissed Lizzy on the neck.

"You look dressed to kill in that new blue shirt I got you. Here's your purse from the other room. Let's get us a booth, huh? I promised Lee and Billy a game of pool before we eat. They get such a kick out of beating me, you know." He hooked her little finger with his, but she held up her glass.

"I want another drink." She downed the last swallow. "A shot of tequila this time."

"Wai-hait a minute." But Jake was smiling, already signaling Frank to pour. He wrapped his arm around her waist and growled in her ear. When he kissed, his eyebrows hunched together into one black furry line. "I'm starved. The processor was down all day again. What say I go order us supper from Pearl while you get your drink, huh?" He moved off before Lizzy could answer and the other workers closed in around her to get their drinks.

Lizzy looked down the length of the bar. Not a face she didn't know, not a voice she couldn't recognize. They all had lasted through the same teachers together, fought in the same Jungle Gym dust and stared out the same sugar-dusted classroom windows, year after year waiting to get out. For most of them, the only big change was graduating from waiting for the recess bell to waiting for the refinery's five o'clock whistle.

There were exceptions—Lizzy's favorite uncle, Sam Waters, for one. Sam had quit his job at the refinery without notice and moved his family eight miles out of town to farm corn. According to Doc Seymour, Sam's wife, Edie, had Alzheimer's. Someone tweaked the back of Lizzy's neck but she did not turn around. The last time she had seen them was at church last summer, and although her aunt had looked fine, instead of bowing her head to pray, she had folded her hands and begun to say her times tables. Loudly. Sam had hustled her out before the service even started, Lizzy's nine-year-old cousin, Ruth, in their wake, her little face stunned with shame. Lizzy missed them, but she never went out to visit their new farm. No one did. Sam had put up a gate on the driveway that he always kept locked.

Frank dropped off a tequila and Lizzy pushed her way between Zene Gercer who was so dumb he failed ninth grade twice, and John Wackett, who never thought to get his crutch out of the way, always reminding you he was just as crippled up as ever. They stopped talking and one of them cupped her ass. They smelled of tobacco and boneblack. Not like Jake. Jake always washed.

She sat in the booth beside Jake's lunchbox. He was leaning over the pool table, Lee and Billy like mirror images on either side of him, and he winked at her before he shot. The juke came on and Harley Barrows in the next booth yelled that he was buying himself five shots, one for every month that Baby Annie had put up with him. Lizzy's jaw tightened. When he started to repeat it, she reached over and cuffed off his hat.

"For Christ's sake, Harley. We heard you the first time."

He swivelled and tried to focus, already grinning drunk, gripping the back of the booth. "Hey there, good-looking."

Lizzy turned her back to discourage him. She watched Frank's dog, Betsy, who was trying to get to the kitchen without getting stepped on. Betsy was deaf and arthritic, with cataracts that made her eyeballs look as if they'd been rolled in sugar dust. She moved forward slowly in a straight line, head low, grimly staring in front of her, stopping, waiting, allowing herself to get nudged and kneed, but never budging off her path. When she made it, Lizzy leaned back and felt fingers wiggle through her hair to her neck. She jerked forward, grabbing Harley's hand, so angry that for a moment she wanted to sink her teeth into it. But he was hiding on the other side of the booth, howling in falsetto "Help! Help!" She batted his hand away, slid out of her seat and into the other side of the booth where he could not reach. "Okay, Harley. Fuck off."

He peered over the top of the booth. "Ooo-hoo," rolling his eyes. "Spitfire." He sank slowly behind the back of the booth. Lizzy picked up her drink and downed it, squeezing shut her eyes until the burn was gone.

Over at the pool table Jake scratched. He was handsome all right, big and dark as an Angus, but gentle, too. He never lost his temper. He didn't drink too much, he didn't gamble, he didn't fight and he didn't use chew. Blue Ribbon stock, Stygo's best, that's what her father had said, that was Jake Loper. Jake would have slit open his soul to make her happy. Even when she told him she'd changed her mind about having kids, the one thing he wanted almost as much as he wanted her, even then he loved her—loved her harder in fact—bought her presents like the turquoise blouse and danced her around the juke.

You had to love a man like that.

Pearl came by with another shot of tequila from Jake and asked if Lizzy had heard who was back in town. Lizzy told her to bring the steak sauce and pushed out of the booth, weaving her way through the crowd to the jukebox. She searched her purse for change, punched 20A and stood with her eyes closed until Frankie finished.

But when she went back to the booth, the sleeve of her blouse caught the sugar bowl and tipped it over, spilling sugar on her steak. The muscles of her jaw clutched and tightened. Over at the pool table, Brice Jopa was bragging to Jake about the horse his father had bought, drawing it in the air with his hands. His sister, Becca, was standing beside him in a new dress, watching his mouth move, looking like she'd given up on her brother ever being smart. Jake was twirling his cue stick and staring at the floor, shaking his head, impressed. Lizzy picked up a fork, turned her steak over, blew off the rest of the sugar and switched plates with his.

If he noticed, he didn't say. He cut up everything into chunks and ate quickly, swabbing up ketchup. He was not the type to complain, especially about food. Billy came by, tipped his John Deere cap to Lizzy and asked if Jake had told her the clubfoot joke yet. Lizzy looked away, but Billy didn't get it. "Well, I can tell you," he said happily. "Scoot over."

"Wait'll you hear it, Liz," said Jake through his mouthful of steak.

"If this is about Frank's niece—"

Billy's grin faltered. "It's just in fun, Liz."

It was not a good joke—none of Billy's jokes was—but

Jake slapped the table hard enough to make the plates jump. "You kill me," he roared. "Where the hell you come up with jokes like that anyway, boy?"

Billy blushed with pleasure. "I thought up that one when Lee and I was over in Sweetwater last Tuesday." He took a handful of fries off Lizzy's plate and began to toss them one at a time into his mouth. "Think she'd like the one about the Yiwa and the sheep farmer?"

"Oh God!" Jake held up his knife and fork like banner poles. "You got to hear it, Liz. Go on, Bill. Tell it the way you told me."

"Sure," said Lizzy. "And eat half my dinner why don't you."

Billy stopped chewing and exchanged looks with Jake. "Naw," he drawled, sliding out of the booth. "Guess I'd better go see what my brother's up to. Nice seeing you, Liz." But as he turned, he ran into Pearl, who was coming with his dinner. Billy told her to take it to the end of the bar, but Pearl had plates all the way up both arms, and with a "Bullshit, buster, you eat where I deliver, or you don't eat," she slapped his dinner down on the table and went on to the next booth. Jake laughed and shook his head and told Billy to sit. He leaned around the corner and yelled at Pearl to bring more drinks with dessert. "Now go on, boy," he said. "If I have to buy your dinner for the pool game you just beat me at, you have to keep us company while you eat it. Right, Lizzy? See, Fiddle? She's smiling. Come on. I want to hear the joke."

"Naw you don't," said Billy, poking at his food, and Jake said "yeah we do," and on it went like that until the third time around.

"Stop it!"

They stopped and looked at her.

"Hon? You okay?"

She took a deep breath and smiled. "If you want to tell it, Billy, just tell it."

Jake grinned. "See? My Lizzy knows what she wants. Go on, Fiddle."

Billy opened his napkin, tucked it into his collar, and poured some ketchup on his steak. "Well sir, there was this Yiwa girl once, 'bout as crazy as a cricket, and one day she seen this big old swarm heading towards Stygo. . ."

Lizzy pushed her dinner away and closed her eyes, trying to relax the muscles in her neck. She heard Pearl come by and move plates around on the table. Coupled with the smell of Red Spot rum, the tequila and strawberry pie were turning her stomach. She opened her eyes and nudged Billy. "Let me out a sec, Fiddle, okay?"

But Billy was in the heat of it and enjoying himself hugely, as he always did when he was with Jake, waving his fork and rolling his eyes and talking through the steak in his mouth. He'd probably forgotten she was even there. She leaned forward and put her hand out, but a woman's laugh rose suddenly clear of the noise, taking her voice with it. She knew who it was without turning around. Willa Moon crowed when she laughed and she could laugh like nobody's business.

"Why, looky there!" cried Jake, craning up to see over the top of the booth. "Liz! Billy! Look who just walked in!" Billy twisted around, mouth open. Lizzy slid back into the corner, picked up her drink and then turned to look.

Willa Moon, standing between the saloon doors in a shiny

blue dress, all slits and seams and blue spike heels, waiting for her eyes to adjust to the dark. Heavy around the shoulders, almost mannish but bony just the same, that was Willa, the same wild-eyed Willa Moon, pushing open Frank's saloon doors and laughing at nothing. Her hair was still black and tangled and long, and she tossed it back with an angry toughness Lizzy knew. A tip of tongue moved slowly across her upper teeth, testing the edges as she surveyed the men at the bar. "Holy hell and goddamn," said Harley. And she still hadn't taken to makeup yet, either.

She took her time, letting them look her over and then strutted across the room to the bar. Sy Peske and Billy Quail were having an argument, perhaps the only two in the room unaware of Willa Moon's entrance. She came up behind them and winged them in by the neck, swaying forward until the three of them touched foreheads. Sy had to grab the bar to keep from sliding off his stool. Billy Quail shrugged her off, smoothed his braid back into place, picked up his spatula, and walked stiffly off to the kitchen, but Willa just laughed and took over his seat. Billy Quail was the only Yiwa male living in Stygo and he liked to say he would never cut any woman—red, white, or yellow—slack, especially if she was beautiful. And Willa was beautiful—though no one would admit it, because she was bad, too.

"Well, people—" called Harley. He took off his new black cowboy hat to smooth down what was left of his hair and eased out of his booth. "Moses crept, Jesus wept, and looks like I'm going to have to put out this fire with a little gunpowder."

"Wait for me," said Billy. The two set their hats and with toes turned out moved toward the bar, noses stretched forward like dogs on a scent.

Frank was standing behind the bar stiff as a poker, his whole face out of control, watching Willa talk, watching her laugh, watching her kiss Sy Peske hello. Lizzy pushed her strawberry pie away and pulled her legs up on the seat. Johanna, with her husband in tow, was moving through the crowd toward the bar, using her swollen belly to get people out of her way. When she got up behind Willa, she dropped Oren's wrist and clamped her hands over Willa's eyes.

"Guess who, Willa," she squawked. "Just guess who!"

Willa pushed Johanna's hands away. They had never been friends. Johanna had called Willa a slut. But a clear, sharp caw of laughter rang out against the mirror. Willa wasn't scared of anybody.

"Aren't we going to go say hi, too?"

Jake was on his feet, holding Lizzy's purse for her. She looked up at him and pointed to the seat across from her. "Just sit, hon, okay?"

Jake sat, eager as a dog. "You and Willa were buddies, huh. Before us." He finished his own pie and started on hers, his eyes on Willa and leaning forward on his elbows to be heard above the crowd. "She looks pretty good," he said.

"What do you mean, pretty good? She looks great."

"I mean, considering what she went through with that kid up in North Dakota."

Lizzy shot him one of her looks before turning back to the scene over at the bar. "He wasn't a kid," she said. "He was as old as you."

Jake cupped one ear. "What'd you say, hon? She's drunk though, you can tell, huh. Why you think she's come back after all that?"

"She's not back." Lizzy's throat felt tight. "She just came to have a good time. That's all." Willa held up her glass and both Sy and Zene Gercer leaned to signal Frank. Billy Fiddle was behind Johanna, shifting back and forth, trying to get in closer. He tapped Johanna on the shoulder but she reached by him, grabbing Oren's wrist, reeling him in closer, and shutting out Billy altogether. Lizzy looked around the room. Everyone was watching. Kwami was behind the saloon doors, peeking over the tops of them, eyes empty and black, chin sharp as an arrowhead.

"Speak up, sweetheart. I can't hardly hear a thing."

"What do you mean," Lizzy shouted, " 'after all that'?"

"Why, her getting mixed up with a psycho—" Jake sounded confused. "The things you told me—what you heard from Johanna. Willa's drinking and whoring around and maybe even getting pregnant—"

"She doesn't know we know that. And it's probably not true anyway."

"Maybe," shouted Jake. "But if it's not, I'll bet Johanna's about to find out."

He was right. Johanna was chumming elbow to elbow between Willa and Fun Harrison, who owned the carnival. Oren stood to one side, looking lost, holding Johanna's pocketbook and fingering his badge. Willa leaned back at something Johanna was saying and let loose another howl.

"So you think she's not back for good," Jake shouted over a Rye Gibson song. "Well, I do. I bet she's back to claim old Harley this time. Think she's heard about him and Baby Annie yet?"

Harley and Baby Annie were planning to get married, but she'd gotten allergic to sugar dust and hadn't been seen at the bar all summer. Harley was ducking past Johanna, jockeying into position. He leaned forward and touched his new brim hello but Willa spoiled the effect by laughing wildly, removing the hat and putting it on her own head. Merle Haggard came on the juke singing "The Same Sweet You." Becca Jopa pulled her brother out to the floor to dance. Brice stared past her shoulder, stiff with shame, still holding his cue stick.

"You ready to go say hi now, find out why she's back?"

Jake's voice was so close she jumped. He was leaning forward on his elbows with his eyebrows scrunched together and his neck stretched up to see better, and when he realized she was staring at him he pulled in like a turtle. Lizzy asked herself if he had known Willa the way the others said they had and then answered herself that it didn't matter. Even if Jake and Willa had fooled around, Willa wouldn't have given him anything she cared about. Besides, Jake wasn't the type. He'd have married her first.

"What makes you so interested in Willa Moon all of a sudden?"

"She was your friend—wasn't she? I mean, isn't it the right thing to make her feel at home?"

"Maybe she doesn't want to feel at home." Lizzy could taste her own breath, sour with tequila. "Got a cigarette?"

"Thought you quit." Jake reached for his jean jacket.

"Hell, I thought you were on a diet." She looked up from the dessert plates and briefly felt awful about treating him mean. She took a Winston from him and watched Willa while he fished for his lighter. Johanna was plowing her way back from the bar with Oren by the wrist, pausing to shout something in Pearl's ear. Pearl turned with her eyes wide and let Johanna pull her away from the bar. They lost Oren in a crowd of men at the jukebox and as they passed the booth, heading for the bathroom, Johanna said over her shoulder, "I don't have a doubt in my mind." The bathroom door closed behind them. Buck Owens sang a song Lizzy didn't like. Couples got up to dance. Becca Jopa was dancing by herself.

"Whoops." Jake blew out the match and searched his pockets for the pack of Winstons again. "Your cigarette's broke."

I don't want it now." Lizzy crushed the broken cigarette into her pie.

Jake shrugged and took her hand. "Okay, sugar. Whatever you want."

"Want to know what I want? You wanna know really?" Reaching out for his shirt. "Do you always have to love me?"

Jake laughed. "Course I do. What makes you think I couldn't?"

"Always and always?" The booth swayed.

"Sure."

"And anytime I want, we just get up and go?"

"Already? But you didn't even say hello to your friend yet."

"I mean out of here. Out of Stygo. Out of anyplace. Anywhere at all."

"Sure, honey. Just tell me what you want."

Lizzy was frightened. "Will we have to answer to nobody then? We don't have to be here unless we choose it?"

"It's always been that way." He was stroking her hand. "You just give the word and I'll see you get it. Anything you want."

"Huh."

"You want to find out about your friend now?" He started out of the booth, but when Lizzy did not follow him he slid back in.

"You look a little tight." He reached for her hand, weaving his fingers through hers, and squeezed. "But like Lee and Billy are always telling me, that's the only way to be on a Friday night, huh."

Johanna and Pearl came out of the bathroom, exchanged looks, and separated.

"Get me my comb, okay?"

The words mucked out, heavy and stupid. His eyebrow hunched together in concern as he handed her her purse.

"Sugar, you shoulda eaten more."

She pushed out of the booth and headed toward the bathroom. The mouse in Shirley's bowl was no longer there and although this didn't bother Lizzy—a mouse was just a mouse—she thought there was something awful about the way you never saw it happen, the way it was there one minute, on its hind feet like a little man sniffing the air, and not the next, while Shirley was always there, always, staring like something dead frozen-grinned at the glass. Lizzy opened the bathroom door but before it shut behind her there was that laugh again, crowing clear and strong as ever. "All right gents," she heard. "Who gets the first dance with Willa Moon?"

■

There were two lights in the bathroom, one broken above the toilet and the other without its lampshade next to the mirror. She took out the comb. Charlie Pride was wailing. The walls were vibrating. She laid the makeup out on the shelf below the mirror and steadied herself against the sink. She used rouge first, then lipstick. Her earring had come loose, but when she closed one eye to focus on refastening it she tipped off balance and bumped against the mirror. The dye job didn't look so hot. In the stark light against the pink wall behind her, her hair looked green. The rouge and lipstick like paint. She made a face, pulling her mouth down at the corners. If she squinted her eyes, she could look like a Roadrunner cartoon, Wile E. Coyote with his foot in the railroad tracks, hearing something coming, turning to face the tunnel. She picked up her purse and hit the mirror. It rattled against the wall.

She went in the stall for the roll of brown toilet paper, tore off long strips, and soaked them under the tap. She scrubbed until the makeup was gone, until her skin was blotched red and raw. Her blouse got wet, drooping a darker blue down the front. She turned her purse upside down, shook the contents out in the sink and opened the door to the bar, this time snaking to the left through the hallway to the kitchen.

Pearl was at the sink in a large pair of yellow rubber gloves, muttering to herself and washing dishes, an open bottle of Red Spot on the counter beside her. When she paused to take a drink, holding the bottle in both hands to keep from dropping it, she shut her eyes and Lizzy slipped around the corner and out the back door.

It was a relief to be away from the noise and out in the street, alone. A cat mewed from the shadows, and out in the beet fields a dog began to bark. If she listened past the noise behind her, she could catch the thrumming of the rocker plates over at the refinery. She stepped off the porch, walked through the alley and started down Bent Street. Jake had warned her against walking home at night. Rattlers liked pavement for the warmth it could hold, which was why there were sometimes snakes out on the highway at sunup. Lizzy walked carefully, her eyes wide against the dark. But nothing flickered or glittered or coiled, nothing in the street at all save her own two feet, pale and thin-looking on the dark buckled pavement.

When she looked up, she found she had passed the trailer. She stopped and turned and looked behind. Under the red neon arrow, the door of the Rockeroy slapped open and two people wandered out in the street. One of them leaned back and howled at the moon and the other one swore. Holding onto each other, they staggered to a truck, pushed and pulled each other in and slammed the door. After a minute, the engine turned over and the headlights came on. With one taillight missing and the other flickering, the truck bounced on a curb and then hurled off into the dark.

Lizzy looked up, a snake fang of a moon tonight, and then she started walking back toward the trailer. Vaguely wanting to be drunk enough to pass it by again, maybe as far as the culvert this time, or the railroad tracks. Maybe out to the truck stop in Sweetwater, or maybe even all the way to Funtown. And in her mind she saw herself on the far side of the beet fields, miles from anywhere, sliding down hardscrabble through ragweed to where the highway stretched out silent in both directions, its blacktop studded in the moonlight with the sleeping knots of lidless and diamond-backed dreams.

T W O

ARMADILLO

ARMADILLO

 Jack says there's nothing out here but a lot of nothing, nothing but a lot of space. He says he likes it that way, all sky and dirt spreading out from one side to the next, with nothing in between but highway and beet fields and arroyos pointing to the little black dots that are us. When we drive, he looks straight ahead. He says you've got to play it as it lays, watch for landmarks, and not want more than what you got to begin with, otherwise you get lost and go blow away like dust. He says if you take what's there to begin with, then what happens won't sneak up behind. That's why he traps the wild dogs that live down in the arroyo. He brings them home and locks them in the old Chevrolet out back. Those dogs are so mean you have to poke food in through a side window with a stick so you don't get your hand bit off. Slobber and dog fur on the windshield so thick sometimes you can't see who's inside, but boy, can you ever hear them when you walk by. Over in town, they try to keep the dogs off with guns or poison, but out here Jack traps them alive. Three years ago, a pack of them busted through Mama Jewell's fence and carried off two pies and her Chihuahua, but none of them will ever come around our place. They know better than to come sneaking around when they hear their friends yowling inside the Chevy.

He has always been my father, but I've always called him Jack. I don't know what I called my mother because she left ten years ago with my baby sister, whose name was Luce. Me, I am Reba, and always have been Reba, and probably always will be, because Jack won't let them re-name me anything else. In town, they all re-named each other—Tom Go, Mama Jewell, Pearl Stiles and the rest—but they will never re-name me because Jack says that the day they re-named our truck stop The Sweetwater, the day the sugar beet refinery opened, that was the same day our water started smelling like farts. Jack says our water will stay that way until they go back to the old name, Platter. Jack says you got to take what's there to begin with because faith is a fool.

But me, I've had dreams about running across the dirt at night, a straight line above the ground, like a light shooting out from behind a just opened door in the dark, streaking out and splitting the dark in two, howling high over beet fields, rock, wire and dirt, out beyond the arroyo and over the lion-lit sky. I've woken up wet, like I'd been running for real, with my legs still twitching in the tangled-up sheet and my hands held out in front and my ears still buzzing. I, Reba, plain Reba, have done this: I've woken up and felt watched.

But I know better than to tell Jack.

Sy Peske's the one who told me my mother was a beauty. Jack says Sy's nothing but a rummy anymore, but I don't mind sitting with him. He told me the whole county fell under a cloud for Jack's sorrow the day she left with my sister, Luce. He said there'd not been a man on this earth with so many tears to cry, not over a woman, not unless it was crocodile tears. Said Jack couldn't even cook anymore, nor take people's money, nor even go to the trouble of locking up at night. "Had to serve ourselves," he said, "cause Jack'd be too busy bawlin' his eyes out." I can't see Jack with such a sorrow as to ever make him cry, but Sy Peske says it's true. All I remember is having to go stay with Mama Jewell, who fed me good but wouldn't let Jubilee, my armadillo, stay with me. I don't remember my mother except that she had a lot of dark hair, and I don't remember nothing about Luce except a naked white thing that slept in Jake's top dresser drawer.

There's a lot I don't remember or that gets mixed up when I do. Things come up at you from all sides out here, things you didn't mean to remember, while other things disappear you never meant to lose. I wouldn't tell Jack, but if I could, I'd tell Sy what my mother's hair smelled like after she washed it. I'd tell him I remember Jack holding hands with her, or Luce, or me, though I don't; or Luce smiling, or the four of us going someplace, all together, maybe to Stygo or maybe to ride the ferris wheel over in Funtown, all of us laughing.

But what I do remember are the things that last all summer and always come back, so you're never sure if they were then or still are. Like looking out from underneath the porch on a hot afternoon at the highway and the dust and maybe a piece of old laundry soap tangled up in tumbleweeds. Or the smell of water down in the arroyo in August, even though there's nothing but sand and cracked mud left by then. Or the smell of empty bottles and rubber out in the heat of the dump by Fiddle's Tit.

But at least I do remember Jubilee as she was then, though she's not coming back like those smells do every time we have a drought.

There hasn't been an armadillo in this town since Jubilee, not for hundreds of years. Sy found her for me one time when he went down to Nogales with some of the carnies from Funtown. Jubilee: claws ahold of my T-shirt in her sleep as we lay nose to nose under the porch. She had a smell to her—all armadillos do—but I can't exactly recall it. Black eyes you could see from the inside out, and fur in her ears. She'd cry like a baby when she wasn't allowed to come with me. She could swim underwater, and when she got excited, she'd jump straight up in the air like a popped cork.

Jubilee was around when things were what they were and that was enough, when you didn't have to remember what to remember or forget.

But then my mother took Luce and left, and Jack sent me into town to Mama Jewell's. When he told me to come back, he said Jubilee'd run away with another armadillo, but I found her out in the dump with maggots in her eye holes. When I brought her to Jack, he went and yelled at me. Said he'd put her in there after she got run over by a truck out on the highway. Said I'd catch disease for touching dead things. Took Jubilee away by the tail and told me to put up or shut up.

And he didn't forgive me either, not for a long time, not till he brought a cardboard box to me and said it was a present. It rattled when he shook it at me. "Come out from under that porch," he said, and when I wouldn't, he shook it at me again. "Take it, Reba. Heed it. I will not have you sad." And then he made me come out and take it, though I didn't want to, though I wanted to hear more first. But his sorrow must have been over by then because I don't remember him saying any more, only flicking off the lid like you might flick a fly off a horse's butt. And there was Jubilee, my Jubilee, with marbles where the maggots had been, with a little pink plastic tongue and all four feet nailed to a board, stiff as Popsicle sticks so she could stand up. Jack stood over me, and when I looked up, his head blocked off the sun. He said: "You will not be sad and soft, Reba, not if you're to stay with me. I will not account for it."

And it was true, though I didn't think so then. I wanted to be sad a long time, show him I could miss Jubilee forever. Didn't want to call the thing in the box Jubilee either. But Jack took to hunting wild dogs in the arroyo all day, and all night blowing the roof off serving free beer to the beet pickers. Sometimes he didn't even close, and sometimes he'd drag out two dogs and stage a fight so the beet pickers'd have something to stick around for, if there wasn't a fight amongst the pickers themselves first. He hardly took notice of me at all. The beet pickers' wives heard about the betting and threatened to close us down if Jack kept it up; but of course, that came to naught because there isn't another place that makes sweet bacon stew like Jack does, not unless you drive all the way to Springer.

Then in August, Mama Jewell in all her God-righteousness came back to get me, saying Jack's was no place for the disadvantaged, holding her nose when she said it and looking like a rusty crowbar out in our parking lot in her widow dress with dust to the knees. Jack was down in the arroyo but I was under the porch, and I told her I'd go to hell in a box first, that if Jack was no good, I was too, that I'd sic the dogs on her if she tried to come get me. I thought for sure she'd keel when I said that—thought I would, too—only she left instead, fists clenched, but scared enough to look back to make sure the dogs weren't following.

I watched her leave from under the porch, and a hot-cold

space pushed under me, making me think of Jubilee, making me want to bust out laughing and bawling at the same time. But I went inside and got the box and set Jubilee out on the counter. Even though the tongue was pink when it should have been purply white, even though the shell was mostly varnish. It seemed to me a right thing to do. I spat on Jack's dish towel and cleaned the dust off the marbles.

And I was right, because that old Jewell bag, as Sy calls her, mostly leaves us alone now, except for what Jack calls her pity gifts: Christmas casseroles Jack feeds to the dogs, afghans we use to plug cracks in the windows. Mama Jewell tells Sy that Jack and me are animals for doing it, but at least she won't be back. And Jubilee's a big hit with the beet pickers now, more than when she was alive and they said she smelled. They pat her head for luck before they place bets on the dogs.

But me, I still think about the old Jubilee. Sometimes on a day I'll look outside and think I see something skitter under a car or around the corner of the porch or behind the gas pump. At night, just as I'm about to fall asleep, she comes flying up from nowhere. Not sixty yards down the highway, not smacked flat as a hubcap and still rolling, not with the truck already a half a mile away and all the little pieces of her popping free. But before all that, when she was just her. I can wake up feeling watched. Sometimes I'll hear the dogs howling out in the Chevy, and other times I'll remember Jubilee's upstairs with all twenty toes nailed to a board. But if I think of these things, I'll fall asleep and find maggots trying to get out behind her eye holes. It doesn't scare me anymore, not much, anymore, but I know better than to tell Jack.

Because of the sugar refinery, there's more people around

now than before. I don't stay under the porch as much because the dust gets up my nose when they stop for gas. Last August Jack got robbed. They were driving a big purple car and when they skidded around in the parking lot like a fish to make their getaway, a piece of gravel nearly put my eye out. The woman was laughing, but Jack says it wasn't at me. He bought a gun, but they haven't been back. Nowadays I sit inside with Sy Peske when he comes by to bum a meal and a drink. I can keep cool by the fan and watch out the window.

There's more tourists now, too. Usually they stay in their car and look at maps while Sy cleans crud off their windshields. Sometimes if there's two or more, they'll come inside. They order burgers or beer. I won't talk if I don't have to. Tourists think the world is made for them, and they think it stops when they drive away again. They think I was born just so they'd have something to look at.

That's why it's different when she comes. She's alone for one thing. Tourists are never alone. And she's younger than me, though not by much. And though I know she sees me, she doesn't try to pretend I'm not there or stare me down. She doesn't look at me, but she doesn't look away, either. She just sort of stands there in the cafe, standing perfectly, looking at things from the side, like a deer when it's smelled you but hasn't decided what to do yet. I watch her and remember the time a real deer got caught in the cafe. I don't remember how it got there, but before Jack shot it, it busted out every window and broke every chair in the place trying to get back out. I think about that, and I sit on my box waiting to see if she'll do the same thing. Because she is like a deer about to bolt, so much like one I'm not sure the story

about the real deer isn't made up in my head.

She's wearing a white shirt and white pants and white strap shoes, and there's no dust on any of it. She's got dark brown hair that moves light through it and skin the color of coffee with a lot of cream spooned in. Not yellowish like Yiwas, or grey like the sugar beet refinery men, or sun-scarred like Jack and Sy and me. Not like anybody around here.

Sy comes in, but she doesn't look at him neither, just swishes her hair and holds out her money and says something I can't hear over the fan. I click it off fast, but she's turning her head to follow the point of Sy's finger out the window behind me, and I have to look down. I look down. I would slide sideways and cross my ankles if I thought she wouldn't notice. But instead, I have a stare-out with Jubilee, who's lying in my lap on her side, legs out like Popsicle sticks. Now that the fan's off, there's a new smell in the room, a smell as dark and thick and sweet as the gardenias the beet pickers bring back from the flower shop in Springer for their girls.

And there's something else. Sy Peske's a dirty old man when it comes to girl tourists, but he's sure not got a lot to say to this one. The screen door squeaks before I can look up again, and then she's standing on the porch, a barrette of silver so bright in her hair it looks scary. Sy and I watch her tiptoe off the porch and around the corner. Sy sinks down on a barstool. "Holy Toledo and back."

He's just talking to himself, so I don't answer.

"If I was a kid, you know, a face like hers could rip my guts out." He chuckles, but he looks hurt. He closes his eyes for a pull of beer. When he opens them, he looks at me. "Think she's pretty, Reba?"

Me, I can't judge. To say she's pretty is like saying a billion dollars isn't much to ask for. She's beyond all that.

"Well, Jack'd say be glad you don't have to look like her." He turns his back like he's angry at me and slams down his beer. "Well, what the hell do we know?" he says. "Maybe your pop's right. Maybe I'm just too old to worry about it one way or another." Even so, we're both watching the door after that. It's like waiting down in the arroyo at dawn for the deer to come out of a patch of sand grass.

We hear Jack first, coming around the side of the house, talking about the dogs. Sy and I look right into each other just before we hear his boot on the porch, and I see Sy's eyebrows shoot up like he's surprised. "Reba?" he says in a funny sort of way, only just then the screen door squeaks. I make sure I'm tucked small and my ankles are crossed.

Jack holds the screen door open for her, but then he thinks better of it and goes first, knocking her with his shoulder. She is maybe just too small to shrink away from him, but I do see her shy, like Jubilee when Jack tried to feed her, and I know it riles Jack. He moves behind the counter. "Come on in then," he says without looking. "Ain't going to bite us, are you?"

And to my surprise, she does come in, and stands directly, perfectly, just like she did before, with that same sideways look. Jack's grinning like a fox. He reaches in the cooler and pulls three beers. He slides one towards her and gives the other to Sy, who's gone still as stone in his seat.

"You don't look it, but if I remember right, you're old enough to drink now, right?"

The way Jack grins when he says it, the way Sy is not looking at her all of a sudden, the way I suddenly know that nobody's going to look at me if they can help it—something is moving towards something, but I can't figure it yet. And her, who nobody's looking at either, except me that is, she exactly steps to the bar and takes the beer.

I watch the light come through the front window, watch it hit the green bottle and pass through, watch it glint like a steel spark off her silver barrette, watch the cream of her neck take it in when she tilts her head so her hair falls back. She has toes and fingernails painted red. Jack calls polish "whore paint." I look down at my hands and then at Jubilee's twenty toes nailed to the board. She holds the bottle in front of her with her painted hands. If I didn't think she'd disappear again, I would close my eyes to shut out her painted hands.

"I'm almost seventeen," she says. It's the first time I've heard her voice, a voice like colors, from light to dark and back again. Even Jack winces.

"So why'd you stop here?" he says.

There is something going on now. His voice is poison, enough to stop anybody. But not her. She's no pretty girl, her. She winds her finger around a strand of hair, winds it until the red is lost in the black. I wonder will she cry or not. Sy's trying to suck the bottom out of his beer. She sucks one side of her mouth and shifts to the side.

"I came to say hi, that's all I wanted."

But Jack starts laughing like he's choking, and that's when I know what Sy's known all along. The word floats up from nowhere. Luce. And I see that I've known it too, all along, known it without thinking it, ever since she walked through that door. Even though I'd planned her to look so much like me that Jack and Sy would have to ask which is which, even though I've looked in the mirror sometimes and seen her, even though all of that, now that she's here, I'm hardly surprised. I am Reba and I will always be Reba; and here is Luce, soft and scared and not like me in a million years.

"Remember Jubilee?" I say. But Jack steps in front and blocks off her view, laughing so loud I can't tell if she heard me.

"A sentimental trip, is that it? Is that what you want?" Jack opens his arms and waves them like sticks, trying to catch his breath from laughing. His noises are huge, rising like a howl against her. "It's the grand tour then? Your mamma, that's what she came for. She burned this place alive, she did. I tell you, she set it afire before she left."

"Jack," says Sy and he waves his tongue but no words come out. I peek around Jack and see her hair's fallen all around her face like black water so you can't see her eyes.

"Guess you don't have to wait, do you," says Jack. "A gal like you's got to see the world. Why, we can show you the front yard and the side yard and the backyard, and the dump, of course, and if you stay around long enough, you might even get lucky—" But his voice cuts off when she swings up to look at him straight on. She's not crying neither, though maybe she will in a moment. But when she looks at him, just looks at him, it's like Jack's looking down a gun barrel. Then she looks straight at me and then at Sy, and then, maybe in mercy, she turns and looks out the door. No, there's not a word in this world can say what Luce looks like when she looks at you.

Sy jumps up. "Lay off her, Jack!" he cries, and his twisted hands shake in fists. "She ain't done nothing wrong. You stop baiting her."

"Baiting her? I ain't baiting her, rummy. I just think if she's

come here wanting to change things, she better find out facts
first."

"For Chrissakes, she ain't come here to find out nothing
or change nothing neither."

"Oh yeah?" Jack's voice rises and cracks like a whip
against the smell that is her. "Look at her then, you old fart.
Look at her and tell me that."

Sy won't look, but I do. He's right. She's changed everything.

"I'll have no part of this," says Sy. "I'm too old and I don't
want it." He looks at me once and then he eases by Luce and
out the door. Luce looks out the window like there is something to look at. Like a deer she is, her eyes flat with panic
and not-knowing. Maybe she'll bolt now. You just can't tell
from looking. Jack finally moves a little so I can see without
leaning. And though it's her he keeps staring at, somehow I
get the feeling it's me he's watching now.

"So what does little Lucille want first. Want to know how
hot it gets here in the summer when the wind stops? Want
to know what happened to your mamma's garden after she
left? Or how about a nice Sunday drive to see what the beet
pickers do? Just last week, there was another swarm. The
whole sky turned black. Think you can handle it with
umbrellas and smelling salts? Your mamma sure as hell
couldn't." He wipes his whole face all of a sudden on his
sleeve, so hard his eyeballs roll to white. "Reba can, though.
You haven't even said hellos with her yet, have you? In fact
if I was Reba, I might feel insulted, getting overlooked by
such a soft pretty thing who calls herself sister. Reba, you
better get up and go shake hands with Luce, because she
don't look like the type to talk to you. She looks like she'd

cut out her own tongue first."

My fingers come up to my face, holding a little bit of fur from Jubilee's ear. "I don't want to, Jack."

Jack breaks out in a grin so wide his jaw could split. His shoulders loosen and he leans back, but his eyes are cold as stone. "Go on," he says. "I'll not have you say I got between you and your sister." He looks at me. "Go."

So I get off my box and try to walk quiet. I would erase her with my eyes, but she will not even look at me, only out the door at all that nothing. I touch her hand. It's cool and light and soft as rain. I would hold it to my neck and eyes. I would hide it underneath my T-shirt to feel its softness there. Luce? I ask. And behind us, there is a funny sort of cry, but when I look around, there is nobody there, only the screen door squeaking closed again.

"Is he gone?"

Oh but her voice is pretty! She looks right at me, and then I follow her, behind, in the smell of her. On the porch, she shades her eyes with one of her painted hands and looks out at all of it and I am beside her. If there was a cloud, if the beets were blooming now, if the sun would go down and turn the sky purple. But there's nothing, nothing but dust and the sign and the gas pump and a car behind it, orange as a tangerine. She's staring at it like she is everywhere else but here. The dogs start up in back and I try to think what to say. Sun burns the skin under my shirt.

"That yours?" Pointing to the car.

"Paulie lent it to me."

I'm afraid to turn sideways and look at her. "Paulie."

"He's my boyfriend."

Boyfriend.

"You getting married?"

"I'm don't know. I expect so."

"I'm going to get married."

"You got a boyfriend?" She looks down at my foot.

"Sure I have." The minute it's out, I feel like howling. I look down at Jubilee. "Remember Jubilee?"

"No." She swishes her hair back so I can see her neck. "Why's he keep all those dogs in a car? Jeez, what a creep. If I were you, I'd run away."

"Jack says there's no place to go." We both look down at my foot again. "This is Jubilee," I say. "Want to pat her for good luck?"

"No." The way she says it, I want to close my eyes and erase her but she steps off the porch. She's craning on her toes, trying to see around the corner, holding back her hair with one hand. "I hate him," she says.

"You don't remember Jubilee?"

"I got to go. Paulie's waiting for his car."

"Wait a minute," I say. "Want to know something? Jubilee used to eat fire ants. That's what armadillos like. I had a time of it catching them for her. But she followed me everywhere and boy could she cry when she was hungry. Only, after you left I had to stay with Mama Jewell who wouldn't let Jubilee come because she stunk, but Jack forgot all about her, about Jubilee I mean, so she ran away and got smacked by a truck right out there. And there she was, the best thing I had." I'm out of breath. I touch her arm. I feel it move under her shirt. "She was full of maggots."

Luce turns her eyes on me, blank. I look up and taste gun blueing in the back of my throat. She points with painted fingernail. "What's wrong with your foot anyway?"

"I was born that way. That's the way it is. That's the way it is and that's the way it is." But she doesn't understand, not her, not in a million years. All at once my eyes do close and my hand is holding Jubilee up, up, up above our heads. And I would smash her on the ground, I would smash them both, but the fingers snap off—pop, pop, pop—and my legs run north while my ears fly south and my arms fall apart like pieces of doll, and I looking up at the lion-lit sky, turn round and round in a body that is not, spinning off like a top, until the sky and dirt slap shut again, until the thread that holds me together snaps, until I flip-flop free, whirling away in space, until the backs of my eyes slam open and fill up at last with pain.

Luce!

I am on the ground and she, she is moving to the orange car, moving like a deer and not once looking back. I see her get in and close the door. Are you coming back? Are you? When she starts the engine, her hair swishes forward, and I can see her neck when she swishes it back. She yells something I can't hear over the engine. Luce! I holler. What about Paulie? I'm out by the gas pump, but she's already turning onto the highway, and after a while she is nothing but a little orange dot against the dirt, and then she is nothing at all. I sit on the ground again. I forgot to tell her about the dreams at night, about feeling watched, about the dust under the porch on a hot afternoon, about the smell of water in the arroyo when there is nothing there at all. I sit and wait but I know she will not come back. Jubilee's marbles, a cover of dust from her car.

I stand up and walk around to the back. The sky's starting to cool from white back to blue and soon it will be orange

and then it will be black. The dogs in the Chevrolet start growling when they smell me. Jack's stick is lying on the hood, still wet. I tap against the windshield with it, and there's a sort of scream and flash of teeth against the window in answer. I lean over and rest my cheek on the hot window. Until they stop trying to get at me, until it's all quiet except for them panting.

I edge over until I touch the door handle. Hold my breath, undo the wire that holds the door closed and pull it open. But there's only two, both as sick and torn as hobo-stew dogs. They curl and crouch in the back and watch me. Go on, I whisper, go on. Surprise on you.

But they're waiting. I turn my back to the Chevy and hold Jubilee and the door tight against my front and wait too. And at the last minute, when I think maybe it's a mistake after all, that's when they come leaping out, all a hurling ball of legs and fur and teeth and tongues, rolling and flipping and colliding in circles when they touch back down, yipping and yapping and then tearing away, hightailing it over the railroad tracks and under the fence and across beet rows, out towards the arroyo without once looking back.

I watch until they disappear, until it's quiet and only kill-deers make noise. Then I close the door and tie it together again. Jubilee, I whisper, and hold her up to me, eye to eye.

I go down to my room the back way through the storm cellar, my ears still humming from the quiet, down to the dark cool crowded pantry where my room is, where things are what they are and that is enough. I set Jubilee on the shelf between cases of beer where she can look out in space with her little black eyes. At first it's hard to get used to the quiet, with all its forever no-yowling that comes in through cracks in the window. But after a while I turn on one side and feel myself going, and then, with my legs still twitching and the heat rising up and my arms already wrapped tight around Paulie's neck, I am there.

THREE

ARROYO

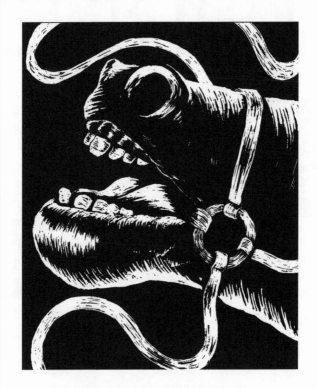

ARROYO

 When I heard Dinah start crowing, I got up and dressed in the dark. Pa Jopa was snoring and my brother, Brice, was grinding his teeth, and from the kitchen it sounded like one person whistling and walking back and forth in the gravel outside. I cut two pieces of bread, wrapped them in a dish towel and put them in my pocket. The rest I left on the table where Brice and Pa Jopa could find it and then I went out to the barn.

The sky was beginning to turn but inside it was dark as ink. Brice's horse, Jacob, nickered to me from the middle stall. I felt past him, put my hand out and Mattie breathed warmth there. Mattie's my horse. She's too old for work—Pa Jopa called her the knacker's gas money—but she has more common sense than all the horses we'd bought and sold put together. Pa Jopa's gray was in the farthest stall. When he smelled me, he shied so hard he slammed into the back wall.

I felt my way over to the ladder and climbed up to the hayloft. Through the cracks in the barn the day was beginning. I crawled over the bales, unlatched the loading door and swung it open.

There was enough light now to make out the corral and the house and Dinah perched on the couch out in the yard, but beyond the yard it was still dark. Behind me something skittered under the hay. I took a seat on the threshold with my legs dangling, heels bumping the outside of the barn, and watched the dark roll back. First our fence line, then Callahan's, then across the flats to the long black cut of the arroyo and beyond that, on the far rim, the pale green of the beet fields where the rest of the world begins. Sammy the milk goat wandered into the yard and settled on the couch next to Dinah. Just before the sun leaked over the horizon, the dirt road leading up to our house turned gold.

When Pa Jopa came out in his undershirt, he peed off the porch, bawling for me and Brice to get up. He'd lost weight since his heart attack and when he turned to go in, his pants hung off their suspenders like laundry on clothespins. A few minutes later, Brice staggered out, scratching his head, hair sticking out in all directions. He's got the same tall, skinny build as me, but he's one year older and his hair is paler than mine, a soft color like shocks of wheat. He started to unbutton, but then he saw me watching and stepped around the corner. When he came back, he did not look up. Through the open door, I could hear Pa Jopa looking for the coffee and yelling at me to wake up and Brice asking questions about the gray. I ate my bread a crumb at a time. Most days I'd be there to answer Brice myself, even if it made Pa Jopa and Brice mad. But today Brice was on his own. Pa Jopa wasn't even listening.

When Pa Jopa was done, he came out on the porch and locked his thumbs in his belt. Brice blew out the door, buttoning his shirt, talking, grinning and still chewing breakfast. Pa Jopa stared until Brice stopped. Brice has nice teeth but Pa Jopa thinks they're too big. He says he's got a beaver for a son. He started across the yard for the barn and Brice followed like he'd been yanked.

They passed under my feet and went inside. I lay back and listened through the floorboards. "You don't have to if you don't want to." The straw hissed as he kicked it aside. "I want to," said Brice. The gray snorted and blew air, banging the side boards. "Where's that sister of yours? Don't she want to watch you ride?"

I held my breath. There was the sharp sound of iron against wood and the gray squealed. "Okay, sweetie pie," said Pa Jopa, "no need to kick the barn down."

He came out leading the gray. I drew my feet up slow and curled around the corner where he wouldn't see me. Everything smelled old and dusty, even my hair. Pa Jopa told Brice to close the gate. I looked up and saw a wasp's nest in the rafters. Pa Jopa yelled for me, but I drew my knees up and laid my head on my arms.

We'd gotten the gray because Doc Seymour had warned Pa Jopa to slow down and start thinking about retirement. Advice like that was to Pa Jopa what gasoline is to fire. The gray was a big pie-faced hammer-head gelding that would just as soon kill you as look at you sideways. Just to get him in our barn, Pa Jopa had had to stun him with a two-by-four. People in town said he'd bought himself his own death, but Pa Jopa just laughed. He said he could get the gray tame enough to rock a baby to sleep. He'd made a bet that within two months Brice was going to ride the gray to town holding a dozen eggs without breaking one. All Brice wanted was to please Pa Jopa. That's all he ever wanted anymore. That's why it had come to this.

Brice was going on about the gray now, how he'd been

honeyfuggling it, getting it used to him and the sound of his voice the way Pa Jopa had told him to do, how he thought the gray was beginning to understand. Pa Jopa told Brice to quit yakking and get on. I closed my eyes and saw everything in the dark.

"Ready?" I opened my eyes and stared at the floor. The gray squealed and there was a scuffle. When I heard the thud, I poked around the corner to look. The gray was dancing along the fence, wild-eyed. Brice was dusting off his butt, only half his mouth smiling now.

"The rope slipped."

"No it didn't. You dropped it." Pa Jopa was right underneath me. His bald spot looked like a fifty-cent piece in a nest of steel wool. He reached in his pocket and then stopped and looked up. His eyes narrowed to slits. "What are you doing there?" I shook my head. He slipped one of his pills under his tongue, pulled his hat on and pushed away from the barn. "Well?"

"Yeah," grinned Brice. "I want to."

Pa Jopa held the gray's head, tame-talking him while Brice got back on. He said something to Brice and Brice nodded, but he was grinning like he hadn't heard.

The gray stood still about half a second and then laid his ears back and took off like he had a squib up his butt. This time Brice landed on his feet. Pa Jopa caught the rein and spat out his toothpick. "That's right," he said. "Ride 'im, cowboy."

It went like that. The gray had a habit of shooting straight up in the air, twisting around and trying to come down right on your face. "Oh, dust don't hurt," said Pa Jopa, helping Brice to his feet. "But it might would help if you tried to stay on." After a few tries, Brice started saying he couldn't. He half sobbed he couldn't. "Got to show him who's who," said Pa Jopa. Looking up at me, he called, "Idn't 'at right, Becca?"

Brice kept trying. The last time, he was grinning like he'd forgotten everything, including the gray. Pa Jopa let go of the lead and when he saw Brice do a back-flip over the gray's tail, he turned away. Brice landed face down and the gray shied off, but then he turned, teeth bared, eyes bugging out. I yelled and Brice was on his feet, trying to make the fence, but the gray was already on top of him. When he tried to roll away, the gray skidded sideways, stretched out and bit him in the neck. Brice yelped, and with a roar, Pa Jopa ran over, pulled him clear, grabbed the lead and punched the gray in the nose.

The gray shrieked, twisted backwards, and ran to the other end of the corral shaking his head. Pa Jopa bent over for his hat. His face was white and he was already reaching for his heart pills. "What do you think you're doing?" he cried when he caught his breath. "All you got to do is ride him, not feed him breakfast."

I drove Brice into Stygo to see Doc Seymour that afternoon. By the time we got back, Pa Jopa was lit to the gunnels. He was sitting on the porch, watching the gray pace out in the corral. He wouldn't look at Brice, wouldn't even let him explain. He said it would take the rest of the summer to undo the damage Brice had done. He said Brice was better off staying in the house and doing dishes with me. Brice had taken five stitches and a rabies shot in the belly, but all Pa Jopa said was that it served him right for being a pussy.

All that week, Brice sat out on the couch in the yard with

his neck wrapped, watching Pa Jopa work the gray. If Pa Jopa looked up, Brice would say something about the gray, how fine and sleek he moved, that kind of stuff. Brice was grinning nearly all the time. He kept saying the only thing he wanted was another crack at the gray. It made me so mad I couldn't eat. One night after Pa Jopa drove into town, I went to Brice's room to tell him to stop lying before somebody believed him again. He wasn't in bed, but then I heard the gray throwing a fit out in the barn and went out to see. Brice was standing just inside the barn door with his back to me. At first I thought he was trying to sweet-talk the gray from a distance, but then I heard the hiss in his voice and I saw the way he was shaking, his body pressed against the siding. He was whispering to the gray what he had told me on the way in to see Doc Seymour, what he was going to do to the gray when Pa Jopa was gone. I listened for a while and slipped back to the house. I never told Brice I knew.

The next afternoon, Pa Jopa put thirteen of my hens' eggs in a gunnysack and went out to the barn. Brice and I watched from the window. When the gray skittered out into the corral, Pa Jopa was on his back, holding the sack between his teeth and snapping the reins. They went out the gate and started off sideways across the flats, fighting each other the whole way.

He didn't come back. By morning we figured the gray was probably down in the arroyo and Pa Jopa was in some ditch. I said he could use the walk home, but Brice just shook his head, saddled up Jacob, and headed towards town. I saddled Mattie and took the shortcut through the arroyo. Brice rushes everything, but even if Pa Jopa had ordered it, he wouldn't take the shortcut. Heights make Brice sick.

Pa Jopa wasn't in the arroyo. Brice found him out on the east rim, lying next to the bridge in a bunch of old barbed wire. Brice couldn't get him free and couldn't find his heart pills, either. By the time Mattie and I arrived Pa Jopa's face was blue and his eyes had rolled back in his head.

I knew he was dead, but I couldn't feel it. That night when I heard Brice crying I told myself Pa Jopa was dead but it didn't make me sad. It didn't make me anything. All I felt at the funeral was shy, and if people hadn't been watching I doubt I'd have felt even that. But Brice, who was always live-ly and gay and always out to please Pa Jopa and always half sick to his stomach because he never could—who had a hundred reasons besides the ones I had to be glad it was over—Brice just stopped. At the funeral he stood at the cas-ket looking straight ahead into nothing. On the way home, he stared at the crack in the windshield, holding his hands in his lap like things he was keeping for someone else.

When we got back, he slammed the door of the truck and went out behind the barn. Because it did not seem right to do chores yet, I opened all the doors of the house to let in the breeze, made myself a sandwich and sat in a chair by the window. Through the back door, I could see the corral and the couch, and through the front door I could see across the bleach flats to the arroyo. A car out on Route 34 caught the sun, but it was too far away to hear. Except for chickens, there was no sound at all. After a while I went to my room and took off my dress. I stood at the mirror, looking at all seventeen years of me, and then I walked around in my slip, feeling how it would be for Brice and me to belong in this house again, feeling the difference of everything and wish-ing I could tell Brice.

But that night the house felt too big. I milked Sammy and then I waited in the kitchen and then I lay out on the couch. The sky was full of stars. Sammy curled up behind my knees and snored through her beard.

In the morning, I found an empty can of beans in the trash and a spoon in the sink. I fed the chickens and milked Sammy and then I made a big plate of sausage and tashbread and carried it behind the barn.

Brice was on the ground with his back against a barrel of sheep dip. There was straw in his hair and his face was streaked. I sat down and put the plate between us. He looked like he wanted to pick it up, but he didn't.

"Aren't you ever going to eat nothing but beans, Brice?"

But instead he pulled his knees up and hid his face in the crook of his arm. "The son of a bitch said it was my fault."

"Sure it's your fault," I said. "It's your fault when it rains and your fault when it doesn't rain and your fault Dinah turned out to be a rooster and your fault Mama died and everything else, too. You should know that by now." I picked up the plate. "Want something to eat?"

"He wanted that horse." Brice sounded ready to cry. "All he ever wanted was that horse."

"I know."

But Brice looked at me then like I hadn't heard. "But that's all he talked about before he died. That's all he damn asked for when I got there—"

"It's not going to help to lose your temper at me. I agree with you. It's better without him."

I started chewing on a piece of tashbread but Brice was still staring. "What," I said. But I knew. When Brice wants something, his face is easier to read than books. I put down the bread. "Okay. What do you want to do about it?"

He turned his face away, picked up a piece of gravel and threw it.

"We got to do something. That's what you're thinking, isn't it? We can't just sit here the rest of our lives."

He picked up another piece of gravel. "Girls," he said, and he threw it, hard.

"Come on, Brice. I don't want to fight, not anymore."

Brice reached for another piece of gravel and lifted his hand but then he stopped, narrowing his eyes at the distance. I looked too, half expecting to see the gray hightailing it across the flats, a rooster tail of dust behind him. But there was nothing, just emptiness, just dead grass and sky all the way to where you can't see. There's part of me that's always known why I stayed after my mother died, but there is another part that will never understand. I thought Brice was thinking the same thing, but when I looked, he dropped his eyes, and I knew all at once that he was not thinking that at all.

"Want to know what I think?"

He threw a piece of gravel. "Not much."

"I think we should kill him." Brice's head jerked but he wouldn't look at me. "He's down in the arroyo on the north end," I said. "That's where he'd go. We just take the gun and run him up one of those blind draws. Bang. Just like we talked about last winter. You and I. . ." He was turning to look at me, so slowly you might think his neck worked on a screw. "Well?" I said. "That's what you were thinking, isn't it?"

It was, I could tell from his face it was, but I knew all at once he couldn't take hearing it. I picked up the tashbread. "Forget it then. I was just trying to help."

"You want me to kill the gray?"

"Cut it out, will you? It doesn't matter to me."

"No, wait," he cried. "You're trying to tell me that the last thing in the world he thought of before he died is worth nothing—" he chewed on the word "—nothing but a hole in the head?"

"I don't have to do this for you." I stood up and started walking towards the house. "Do whatever you want with that horse," I said over my shoulder. "I don't want to help you. You'd probably just shoot yourself in the foot anyway."

"So. She's lost her temper." It was Pa Jopa, bitter and cold as lake ice, but I heard the crack in it, heard Brice underneath. I spun around on my heels.

"For your information, that horse isn't worth a ding and you know it and even if you want to bring it home alive you can't do it without me. You know you can't."

He got to his feet. "I don't have time for this shit."

I waited until I heard the door of Pa Jopa's truck open and then I yelled and ran after him.

"I've got just as good eyesight as you," I yelled, slapping the hood, "and I'm better at tracking. You have to let me help. You know you do."

He stared out the windshield, tightening his mouth over his teeth. "You just said you wouldn't help."

"I won't if you keep talking like Pa Jopa."

"I'm not talking like anybody." He snatched the door away from me and leaned out the window to tie it shut with the baling wire. "Besides. I don't need your help. I can get somebody in town."

"Like who?" Brice reached under the seat for the keys but I grabbed the door handle. "Give me the name of one person who'll help you bring back the gray if I don't."

"Frank Stiles." He knocked my hand off the door and started the truck.

"Right," I said. "Good choice. Frank Stiles. Better yet, how about Jake Loper? He really knows his horses."

Brice threw it into gear and backed up. Our chickens squawked and flew around the yard.

"Don't you leave me here," I said. "I'm warning you."

He paused and looked over at me. "Buck up, Sis. We all got to get tough sometime." He made a sucking sound at me and then turned out of the yard, nearly clipping the tail feathers off Dinah. I watched the truck go down the road until it hit Route 34 and turned left, heading towards Stygo.

"You damn Brice," I yelled.

Frank Stiles and Jake Loper both said the gray was better off with a bullet between the eyes. I could see it on Brice's face when he roared back in the yard that night. He stormed past me, saying we'd be going in the arroyo tomorrow from the south end. "The shortcut's too steep for your nag," he said.

But Mattie and I'd used the shortcut not three days before to look for Pa Jopa. She always did fine on steep trails. Nothing ever flustered her except maybe a burr under her saddle. I could have told Brice this. I could have reminded him about the last time he used the shortcut with me and how he'd managed to get down. But I didn't. I said "What- ever," to his back and went out to milk Sammy.

By the time I was awake, he had already packed our lunch and fed the animals. From the window I saw him out in the yard, his hat pulled low and Pa Jopa's red bandana tied around his neck. He looked like he'd been up all night again. I ran to get ready, afraid he would change his mind about me coming if he had to wait. Pa Jopa's gun was gone but I wasn't about to ask if he'd hidden it from me or packed it. I went out in the yard and took Mattie's reins from him. He didn't even say good morning.

The day was soft-pawed and cool from the night before and we walked single file, Brice on Jacob opening the gates, and me on Mattie closing them. Once we were out on the flats I started feeling better. I felt like talking, and I wanted Brice to feel like talking, too. I mentioned how green the beet fields looked on the far rim and the killdeer's nest I'd found in the chicken coop. I told him the way old Mattie was eyeing Jacob's butt, and when we scared up a coyote taking a dirt bath, I said the Yiwas believed that meant rain. "Did you know that, Brice?" But he wouldn't answer. An hour later when we reached the mouth of the arroyo and started up into the draw, I said we should come here more often because it used to be one of our favorite places to go. "We can do just about anything we want now," I called to him. "We can even buy a dog if we want to." He wanted a dog. But instead of being nice about it, he snapped around in his saddle.

"How come you talk so much?"

"Jeez, Brice. What's wrong with talking?" I said. But he only kicked Jacob on ahead.

I didn't talk again until I spotted some tracks off to the right heading up a narrow draw. Brice missed them and I told him to stop but he didn't even slow down. So we rode until he was hungry, both of us angry, picking our way through the fallen boulders, up one blind alley and down another, and I didn't say another word.

It could have been the heat or the silence between us, but after we finished lunch we lay down in the shade and fell asleep. One minute I was listening to the horses sighing and stamping away flies, sounds echoing off the walls around us, and the next minute I was leaning on the bar in town, watching that woman, Willa Moon, and feeble-minded Kwami, playing cards over in a booth. I kept asking what they were playing, kept saying I wanted in, but neither would answer. Then Pa Jopa's hat came flying over the top of the saloon doors like someone had thrown it from the front room, and when I got off my stool to get it, I heard the sound of galloping. I shouted and ducked down between the barstools, felt the thundering under my hands as the gray came busting through the doors. I looked up in time to see him and Brice both crash by in a whirr of gray mane and tail, Pa Jopa's hat caught in the wake. I held out one hand to grab hold of it but just as I was about to, I heard Brice's voice.

"You crying?"

"I am not." I was holding my breath. The cliffs rose straight up over us like the walls of a room with no roof, curling over at the top. "I had a dream, is all."

"I thought you said you never dream."

"I never do." The edge of a cloud touched the sun and rolled off again. The arroyo was dusty and still. I looked over at Brice. He was lying on his back with the bandana over his face. "Want to hear it?"

"No."

I sat up and watched him lying there. Brice used to tell me all his dreams. "I know where the gray is."

"Uh-huh."

"It's true. I saw tracks."

He jerked up, his face pink from sleep. "What?" His

cowlick stuck up like a thorn.

"We crossed them."

"What? How come you didn't say nothing?"

"I did. I said so back there at the first fork."

"God." He fell back. "First you say you don't want to help, then you do and now you tell me you've known all morning we were going in the wrong direction."

"I tried telling you—"

"Well try harder." He sat up. "And from now on, don't lead me to think you're doing one thing when you're doing another."

"Look who's talking."

He got up and pulled Jacob to him. "Let's go."

The ground was rough and bad for cantering, but Brice did not slow down until we got back to the fork. "So where are they?" he shouted. I nudged Mattie ahead of him and pointed. He drew up, cussing under his breath, and squinted at the ground. His lips snapped back from his teeth and then he whacked Jacob and they took off following the tracks into the split. "You better wait for me," I yelled. "Brice?" I gave Mattie a swat with the rein and we went after him at a trot.

He couldn't have asked for a better place to catch a horse. Two hundred yards and the walls widened out and then circled around an open spit of sand as bright and flat as a silver dollar. The gray was up at the far end under the shade of an overhang, standing there like he'd been waiting for us to find him all morning. His saddle was gone and he stood hock-deep in a slime pool, green water dripping off his muzzle, one rein looped over his ear. Pa Jopa'd scratched whip-marks all over his flanks and there was a nasty-looking hole in his neck, probably from barbed wire. His mane was matted with burrs and sticks and bits of eggshell. The air was so still it made me feel light-headed, like I'd had too much sun and too little sleep. When he caught our smell he stepped forward, shivering flies away. I eased Mattie up behind Jacob.

"Brice?"

He turned in his saddle, leather creaking. "Been back there fixing your hair, or what?" His lips twitched at the corners but he kept them closed over his teeth. When he shook out the first rope, the gray leapt off to a trot, circling the draw, flashing his tail and wagging his head, trying to find a way out.

Jacob is quick on his feet and no matter what Pa Jopa said, Brice can throw as well as anyone, but that gray knew something about slipping a noose. He held his head high to keep from tripping on the reins and ducked low for every throw. He paced back and forth along the wall, snorting and stirring up the dust under the sand. Every time he tried to bluff Mattie, I held her firm and shouted until he wheeled the other way.

After a while you could barely see for the dust. Jacob and the gray were lathered up and Mattie was beginning to cough. I told Brice to give me one of his ropes, but he wouldn't.

And then all of a sudden he had the gray by the back foot. It squealed like a girl and dropped sideways and the noose began to slip but the gray got his foreleg caught in the rein and while he was trying to shake loose, Jacob threw himself backwards and the line went tight. Brice threw a neck line before the gray could roll, anchored it on the horn, slipped off Jacob and ran forward. "Use the third rope. Get his front feet. Front feet," I hollered. But instead Brice ran to the

arroyo wall, picked up a rock the size of two fists, ran back
to the neck line, waited until he saw an opening and then
jumped forward, yanked the gray's head close and cracked
him on the forehead. The gray grunted and dropped. Even
Pa Jopa might have been impressed. Brice nudged with his
boot and when nothing happened he eased off the leg rope,
leaned over and blew on the grey's face. Then he stepped
back and whistled for Jacob to step forward, jerking hard on
the neck line. The gray swung his head until he had enough
slack to breathe and lunged to his feet. We waited, but the
gray just stood there, head down, mouth open, nose flared
like china cups, blowing hard.

Brice dropped the rock and edged forward, gathered in
the gray's rein, and backed slowly towards Jacob. His shoulders were set stiff as fence posts and the whole back of his
shirt was wet. He swung up on Jacob. "I got him," he said.
The walls around us echoed it. Jacob shook the dust out and
a stillness fell, with only the sound of us breathing inside it,
all of us watching the gray. A cloud rolled over the sun.
Shadows ran down the side of the draw, and it was cooler.

Brice started to coil his ropes. His hands were shaking. I
got off and went to help.

"He's ours now," I said. "You did it, Brice. He just wham
gave up when he saw that rock."

He turned his head and looked at me. "Ours?"

Then he looked away and asked me to fetch his hat. I did-
n't know what to do so I went and did that and he took it
without thanking me. I got on Mattie and he went by us
into the split, not once looking back, yanking the gray
behind him.

For a moment I felt as lost as if he had sealed the split

closed forever. I looked around at the walls and the slime pool and the place where he had dropped the gray in the sand. All of it quiet, settled again, even the flies gone someplace else. Then I looked up and saw clouds over the top of the north wall, banking up on each other. "Come on, Mattie," I said and we trotted back out through the split.

Brice had stopped at the fork to get out his jacket. "We better get out of the arroyo," I said. "There's rain coming." Brice didn't answer. His whole face was different, shining and hard. He jerked the gray's rein and turned Jacob south.

"Brice? Going south is the long way out. We got to talk about this."

He kicked Jacob to walk faster. "Sorry," he called. "I don't have time to babysit."

The thunder came from the west first. It sounded like someone pushing heavy furniture across a wood floor. I slapped Mattie into a trot. Brice did the same with Jacob.

For a time we didn't talk. Where it was smooth we trotted, but there were too many places where we had to hold back and pick our way. The thunderheads were coming in purple and green now, with high silver crowns. The gray was getting skittish, snorting and crowding up behind Jacob, making him skittish, too. I thought of the times Brice and I had gone out to the rim of the arroyo after a storm and seen trees and car parts from Stygo floating by, nights when we listened to boulders tearing loose and knocking into each other, moving under the water. I found myself leaning forward in the saddle to get Mattie to move faster.

At the main fork the first breath of wind whispered down the walls, loosening the dust off the coyote tobacco. Brice stopped, tilting back to look, mouth open, and turned to me. "For chrissake, will you hurry up?"

"Mattie can't go any faster." I drew up so I could see his face. "We should take the shortcut up the cliff. If we keep going south we won't get out for another hour. The short-cut takes twenty minutes."

Brice wet his bottom lip. "The shortcut's too steep for the horses."

"I used the shortcut with Mattie three days ago," I said. "It isn't that bad. If we walk the horses, we can do it. Even if the rain starts before we get to the top, we'll still be off the floor of the arroyo."

"Dumb." He nudged Jacob ahead of me. "Dumb, dumb."

I stood in my stirrups. "If you can't do it, then I guess that leaves four of us who can."

He snacked Jacob to a stop. "What are you trying to prove?"

"What am I trying to prove? What about you?" There was a crackling of thunder, closer now. I looked up and wheeled Mattie around, heading her north up the draw.

"Wait a minute," he cried. "How do you expect us to get the gray up a trail like that?"

"Hey. It's your horse. Remember?"

"Leave him?" he yelled. "Is that what you're saying? Or should we just push him off the edge?" Then his voice cracked. "He's mine," he yelled. "Mine!"

But I did not answer. There was no point.

We got off our horses at the base of the trail. Brice tied Jacob's reins to his saddle horn, slapped him on the butt, and sent him ahead on his own. Thunder rolled to the west. The mesquite at the top of the cliff rattled against the wind, but in the arroyo everything was still. Brice was staring up.

"Don't worry," I said. "You won't get height-sick."

"Shut up. I'm not worried." But he was. He turned away and yanked the gray forward, his face as white as an egg.

We started up single file, Brice leading the gray by the bridle and me leading Mattie. When the trail began to narrow, we strung a rope between us to fence the gray in against the cliff. "Like a guardrail," called Brice. "So if he gets spooky, he won't shy near the edge. All we got to do is snap it a little." He licked his bottom lip and showed his teeth. "Just a little. Not enough to spook him. Like this. So he can feel it if he gets—"

"I know, Brice. Let's go."

The trail rose fast at first and then leveled out, winding in and out of the cracks along the wall. Brice was trying to honeyfuggle the gray and pull him forward at the same time, but when thunder sounded, the gray's butt tensed iron and his head swung high, feet skuttling sideways. "There you come now," said Brice, "come on now, sweetie pie, that's right." "Ye-e-s, master," I whinnied. But as we edged past the first narrow in the trail, I saw in Brice's face what he was going through, and after that I kept quiet, shoving the gray's butt forward whenever he started to balk, letting Brice talk all he wanted. He was trying to sound like Pa Jopa, but it was finally hitting me that Pa Jopa was dead. It was there inside Brice's voice, growing louder as we moved higher up the cliff, and now for the first time it was inside me, too.

When we came to the outside bend where the cliff begins to sheer off, a gust of wind reached down the side of the rock and lifted the hair straight up the back of my neck. The gray laid his ears flat with a snort and Brice and I flicked the guide rope at the same time. It snapped the gray's belly like a fly swatter and he shied sideways away from the edge. "Jesus." Brice had himself braced against the rock. Sweetie, Sweetie, good boy. He looked out over the edge and then past the gray's shoulder at me. "Hey, Becca?" He was trying to control his face, trying to make it do what he wanted.

"What?"

"Just up ahead there's a place wide enough to turn around."

I leaned out over the edge of the trail to see up ahead. "God, don't do that," he cried, and I could hear it in his voice, in the air all around us. More real than the smell of horse or sweat or lightning strike or even the coming rain. Pa Jopa was dead. Brice was pressing himself against the side of the cliff, his face white, the gray's rein in one fist, guide rope in the other. "We can't go back, Brice." And because he needed me to say it, "You can do this. It's only a storm. Just don't look down again till we get to the top."

The rain started in fat, heavy, slow drops. At first the gray moved forward, shivering and eager as we were to get out, but when the trail turned from gravel to bedrock, he began to spook again. Brice tried to work him down and I tried to keep them moving forward but it didn't do any good. For every step ahead, the gray was dancing two back, yanking Brice with him, hooves clattering on the rock. It started to rain harder and then to blow. The rocks turned dark and slippery and the gray started weaving sideways and back and forth between the guide rope and the cliff, swinging his head to pull free. Beyond Brice I could see the trail rise and curl around a corner with nothing but a view of the whole sky, seasick and rolling. The gray slipped and bumped against the wall and then took a jolt backwards, knocking me into

Mattie. I yelled, feeling slack in the guide rope, but Brice yelled back, "Tighten your end," and I did, watching the line harden again and press into the gray's side. "Now hold it there," called Brice. "Don't move."

He was trying to blindfold the gray with Pa Jopa's bandana. He was making one knot under the jaw and another behind the ears and when he got it, the gray staggered back on his hocks and then eased off, trembling. Brice yelled something. "What?" but a bolt of lightning blew it away and I crouched back against the rock, feeling the thunder coming through it as if the earth was cracking open. I held my breath for it to end and all I knew anymore was that I had Mattie's rein in my right hand and the gray's guide rope in my left and though I could not see or hear him anymore, I could still feel Brice on the other end, raging against the gray, snagging the line tight.

When the thunder ended I stood up—"Okay, Brice, move"—but another strike popped to the north, snaggling across the east wall of the canyon. Brice and I leaned into the cliff, yanking the guide rope against the gray. It would have been just right, but because the gray was blindfolded, the snap spooked him. He screamed and shot forward and Brice called out and hit him in the nose. The gray reared, high this time, and I looked up to see the red bandana flying off like a bird. Brice yelled again and we pulled the guide rope tight as the gray came down on his forefeet. He was twisting around to see, trying to back off, swinging his big club head side to side, his nose and mouth stretched open, his eyes rolling to white. The rain began to pour and another strike came and Brice shouted, "I have him," but I knew he did not. I could feel it in the guide rope, I could see it in the muscles of the gray's flank as they began to gather, bunching under the wet skin. "He's getting ready," I said. "Move away. Let go." But Brice didn't answer. "Let go," I called. But I understood, I caught it in his face, in the way his eyes turned to mine and the way his mouth opened when the gray leaned towards the edge and we snapped him back. Brice couldn't let go and he couldn't move away, he couldn't because he wouldn't, not anymore, because it was his horse now. I stepped forward, gathering in the guide rope and leaning into the rock, and behind me Mattie stepped forward too. She stepped forward and put her nose against my neck and sighed.

So patient, so sensible, so sick and tired of the whole thing. Brice couldn't let go. I looked down at the guide rope in my own hand and I looked up at the gray's flanks, the wet tail where it clung to the leg like an iron-colored vein, then down the leg to the hoof, only a little thing carrying all that weight beneath the muddy fetlock, only a thin pink little hangnail of a hoof, fumbling for balance on the slippery rock. I watched it, I willed it, I made it move with my eyes, and when I saw it rise and jab as the gray rose up, twisting to get free of Brice, I willed it to come down on nothing and opened my left hand. The guide rope cracked the air like a whip and there was the sound of the gravel edge giving way. I could hear the gray shrieking, but when I opened my eyes he wasn't there. I searched Brice's face, pale and open wide, I lifted my hand to him to show him it was empty, and then I fell back against the cliff and listened through the rock.

When the sound stopped, I opened my eyes. The wind was blowing against us, but the rain had eased up. Brice was pressed against the cliff with his whole body, still holding his end of the guide rope. I edged up next to him and he turned his face away, but I slipped my arm around him and pressed myself against him and us against the rock. "It's me, Becca," I whispered. My lips touched the top of his ear and I tasted his hair, wet in my mouth. When he turned his head, he rubbed his lips against the rock, trying to say something. His throat was as pale and delicate as a girl's. It fluttered against my cheek.

FOUR

CORSAGE

CORSAGE

The porch is the best place to be. It used to be that under the honey locust was best, where even when the afternoons were white-hot, the air smelled blue and green. But since Baby Annie's come, I haven't been back there.

From here, though, from this porch swing, I can know everything. I can know what's going on right now in the kitchen and the parlor and the upstairs and the hallway that ties all the rooms of this house together, and I can know what's going on out in the street, too. Where Harley Barrows will stop his car when the crickets start, where he'll toot his horn and whistle hello to me if I'm still here. Tonight he'll smell like linen and limes instead of gasoline. He'll have that Camaro tuned up like a cat, and best of all, Mama Jewell says he'll bring a gardenia with him. I've never smelled a gardenia, but Baby Annie says it's her favorite flower and Mama Jewell says it leaves a trail of beauty behind it, so I guess that must be so.

Baby Annie's in the bathroom with the door locked. She's been in there all afternoon. I have to use the bathroom again, but I don't mind waiting. Not for Baby Annie.

Mama Jewell is in the kitchen. She loves to cook, but today, mixed up with the smells of her and her cooking oil and zinnias and all the other smells of this house and this thick after-

noon heat, I smell Spraystarch. She's told Hallie and me she's too busy to breathe. That's why I'm on the porch—because of Mama Jewell and the gardenia. Baby Annie's dress is taffeta, and it rustles when Mama Jewell turns it.

"You know it'll break everyone's heart if you move out of Stygo after you're married." She's shouting on account of the bathroom door being shut. "I realize things are awfully backward around here for you, Baby Annie, but I've been thinking if Harland wanted to, he could move his trailer into the backyard. I wouldn't mind. Better yet, we could fix up the back bedroom where Mr. Peske and I used to sleep," she says. "Harland seems to like that room, don't you think?" Mama Jewell stops to listen. "Darling? You could open the door. It's not like we're strangers. Besides, I don't like the idea of closed doors in my home. They make me feel lonesome and mean. You hear me?" Then she sighs and starts again, rowing back and forth and back and forth over the taffeta. "Oh, Baby Annie!" she cries. "With you in this peach-colored dress, that poor boy won't be able to take his eyes off—"

"Don't call me Baby Annie."

"What, Baby Annie?" she says. But I know she's listening for something besides Baby Annie's answer, and I know what it is, too. "Hallorie?" Mama Jewell sets the can of starch on the counter and crosses the kitchen. The linoleum floor has grown soft in the summer's heat and her sneakers squeak. She crosses the wood floor in the hall to the front parlor, where the rug is thick enough to grab in bare toes, and I feel more than hear her cross to where I know Hallie's hiding behind the couch.

"What are you up to?" she says. "What have you got

there? Oh—Hallorie!" Back to the hallway, back to the kitchen, to the broom closet. "You think I enjoy this? You think I like cleaning up after you six times a day?" The vacuum tubes ding against the closet walls as she pulls them out. Then she gives a yip and tubes go clanging and banging everywhere.

"For God's sake!" she cries. "Why do you have to sneak up on people like that, Hallorie? You want to give me heart failure, or what? What? Why are you always at me? And what's that in your mouth?"

I shake my head. Days like this Hallie can be so bad.

"How many times have we talked about calories?" says Mama Jewell. "How many times have I told you? Come on. Spit it out. Here, Hallorie. Right here in my hand." Steps and a clank in the wastebasket. "Now go," she says. "Go out to the porch with your stepsister or something. She's probably lonesome out there. Don't you think?"

Mama Jewell picks up the tubes and rolls the vacuum cleaner out into the kitchen, across the wood in the hall, the rug in the parlor. I don't like vacuum cleaners. They take over everything with their sound and then they take it away. The wheels squeak like baby mice caught by the tail. I'm glad Hallie's coming outside. She doesn't like vacuum cleaners either.

What she does like is sneaking up on people. She doesn't care whether you're blind or not. But she never wins. This time the smell of chocolate tells me, and the way Tip starts whacking his tail on the porch in welcome. But mostly it's a knowing I all at once get. You don't need eyes for that. "Hallie," I say and catch hold of her fat-soft hand holding something.

 CORSAGE

It's a cattail from the river, an old one, crusted hard on the outside, only she's broken it open to let the silk out. The stem is smooth and cold and it smells like the river. She holds the silk under my nose and slides her face against the back of my neck. And even now, with the vacuum blasting in the parlor, Hallie's hum sinks down inside me. It feels like my stomach growling. "Hallie," I say. She knows I don't like vacuum cleaners.

■

Hallie's never talked. When they first brought her here, she didn't even hum. She was so skinny back then, her skin felt like pink ribbon wrapped around bone, and all she could do was sit behind the stove and poop on herself. Mama Jewell was about to give up on her and make Sheriff Whatly and the social workers take her back. Later, when Hallie got better, Mama Jewell said she'd known all along that Christian love and patience would do the trick. But that's a lie. The truth is, Hallie got better because of Tip. One day he went to her so sure she would scratch under his harness for him that she did. That was the first day she made noise. Only a little noise, a hum down deep inside of her, and only when Tip came to her. But then it got stronger and she started crawling, and then tiptoeing and walking, and then running, too. And nowadays her hum never stops and neither does she, not until late at night after everybody else is asleep. Now, even if Mama Jewell orders her to stand still and be quiet, Hallie can't. She hums through her food and through her afternoon naps, and even when she holds her mouth shut with both hands, trying to please Mama Jewell, still there is that hum. Like a bumblebee living down in her throat, the big fat slow kind that floats around Mama Jewell's parlor in the thick heat of an afternoon. It's a lot more touch than sound.

■

When Mama Jewell's done, she winds up the cord and wheels the vacuum back to the kitchen. She crams the tubes and brushes in the closet and then she takes out the air freshener and goes back to fill up the parlor with smells. Hallie lets go and sinks down under the swing. Tip groans when she scratches him the way he likes best.

Baby Annie says Tip is the ugliest dog she ever saw and Mama Jewell tries to keep him out of the house, so I guess that must be so. But Tip can't help it if he's losing his hair. He thumps his tail on the porch when Hallie slides his water dish closer.

It's a Tootsie Roll she's got, I can smell it melting in this dead, still heat. She opens one for me and two for herself, but I give mine back. I don't need it. I'm on Baby Annie's Seven Day Beauty Plan. "Maybe I'll eat it later," I say. But I won't. Hallie lays her head on my foot, puts her arm around my ankle and pushes Tootsie Rolls in her mouth. When Tip's done with his, she unwraps two more for him and two for herself. With her mouth so full she has to breathe through her nose. And still through it she hums.

Her socks are stuffed with Tootsie Rolls—that's why she wears socks—and I know her hat and shirt and pockets are, too. Nowadays they always are. Mama Jewell says it's sickening. When Hallie first came, Mama Jewell tried to think up ways to make her eat, but now all she does is try to think up ways to make Hallie stop. She says if Hallie watched her diet, she'd have a face nearly as beautiful as Baby Annie's. But Hallie likes candy too much. She's backward. Mama

Jewell says it's hopeless.

And it is hopeless. Hallie has a hole of hunger in her that nothing will ever fill up. It makes her itchy and quick and sometimes it makes her smell sour. It makes her hurt and sometimes it makes her steal. When it gets bad, it changes her hum—till it's not just one big bumblebee living down in her throat anymore, but a whole swarm of little bees squeezed up behind her teeth and trying to sting through the cracks. When it gets bad she pulls her lips back and runs around the house bumping into things and falling down. Then if she wants, I'll give her all the candy she can eat. Like today, when I feel it building in her. Because I know how it is, how the things you've lost are the only things they remember to talk about, day after day after day.

■

I hope Baby Annie's finished in the bathroom. I hope she's standing up and flushing and pulling down her slip and just leaning a little to unlock the door. I hope she calls Mama Jewell soon and says "If Christina wants to, she can use the bathroom." I don't mind waiting. I don't. But it is hot out here, and this time I have to go. I really do.

■

A lot has changed since Baby Annie. Now there's the new rug in the parlor and the sachet in the coat closet and the lock on the bathroom door. Nowadays, Mama Jewell wears powder and lipstick and sometimes, when she thinks no one will notice, Baby Annie's perfume. Now every Tuesday, Hallie and I have to go with Pearl Stiles while Mama Jewell takes Baby Annie for voice lessons. It used to be that Mama Jewell hardly ever left the house unless it was to take Hallie and me to see specialists in Mason City, but now Pearl says she wonders some Tuesdays if Mama Jewell's coming back. Pearl Stiles is okay, except she won't let Tip in her house. It makes Tip fret, but Pearl says her cats don't like dogs. She can't let us outside to be with him, either, because she could never forgive herself if something happened. Which is what Mama Jewell used to say all the time about Hallie and me. At first, I was glad she quit saying it. But it's one thing to want to be alone and know you never will be, and a whole other thing when you all at once are.

So it's no fun hiding under the honey locust from Mama Jewell anymore. Hallie doesn't understand. She's always at me to sneak away. But somebody has to be Baby Annie's look-out, and it won't be Hallie because all Hallie cares about is Tip and candy and me.

■

Back when Baby Annie first showed up with all her beauty books and swimsuits and diets, I hated her. I sat out on the porch just like this, and I hated Baby Annie all day long. Worse than I hate vacuum cleaners or heat waves or strangers who pat Tip without my permission. Worse than darkness or social workers or Mama Jewell's air fresheners. Mama Jewell told Hallie and me that Baby Annie was a gift from Jesus to prove beauty comes to those who suffer; but all I knew was that, with her here, it was like I wasn't.

At night it was worse. At night the smell of her coating my eyeballs and teeth and the insides of my nose woke me up. I'd hear Mama Jewell dreaming in one bed and Baby Annie in another and Hallie behind the stove downstairs or under the couch or somewhere else I don't know and all the other beds folded up and put away because now we are the last ones, and I'd get lost because out of all of it, I couldn't

hear me. Things came unstuck those nights. Sometimes the closets opened up and the beds unfolded and came out into the dark. Other times it was my head that opened up and unfolded, floating around above my bed, bump bump bump against the ceiling. But either way, the dark inside me mixed with the dark all around the beds until everywhere and every one of us was dark. Like a mouth that will never stop swallowing, like a hole in the world that everything, living and unliving, beautiful and unbeautiful, sleeping and unsleeping, falls into. Dark and dark and dark. And even if Tip came to me then, creeping up on my bed in apology and inching his way up to my face until the sad wet cold of his nose touched my chin and breathed warmth there—even then, I wasn't always sure I was there, too.

Hallie knew how I felt, but she couldn't hate Baby Annie, any more than she could hate Tip or me or anyone else. Tip knew too, in a different dog-way, but the same too, because late at night he'd go off through the house by himself. Listening to the dark, uneasy, I know, sniffing at cracks under closet doors, around cabinets and laundry piles. Like he'd lost something, only he couldn't remember what it was or where he'd lost it. But it was me he went looking for on those nights when he nosed around under Baby Annie's milk breath and beauty guides and lists for Mama Jewell, me he went to find.

At first, I thought Sheriff Whatly's social workers had ordered Mama Jewell to please Baby Annie—just like they had ordered Mama Jewell to put Hallie on a diet and close her in the bedroom when she hummed, just like they had ordered Mama Jewell to be firm with me about independence. I figured Mama Jewell would get sick of Baby Annie and send her away, which is what happened to a few others I could name. But when nothing happened, when Mama Jewell acted as if it was a miracle every time Baby Annie came down to breakfast, I caught on. Mama Jewell wasn't getting orders from anybody. Mama Jewell was just being smart.

Because Baby Annie is beautiful. Not just nice or sweet or brave—things they tell Tip and Hallie and me.

Baby Annie is *beautiful*.

And when you are beautiful, the rest doesn't matter. It leaks out of itself. When you are beautiful you don't need anything, but everybody needs you, and if you go away, you leave a hole behind.

Which is why we're so lucky to have Baby Annie. We never want her to leave. Mama Jewell says Harley worships the ground Baby Annie walks on, and now so do I, along with everybody else. I'm not stupid.

I try explaining it to Hallie, but she won't listen. She's a good kid, but she's hopeless. Mama Jewell says so and I know so. Hallie eats too much and messes the house and won't take baths or comb her hair. She doesn't want to learn. She has eyes to see what Baby Annie is, but she acts like Baby Annie is nobody different. Sometimes she makes me furious. Because one of these days Mama Jewell will say enough's enough, and Hallie will end up going back to wherever she came from, and she'll wonder why, and I won't be there to tell her. Because I'll be here, probably on this very same porch, and I'm the only one who cares.

I wish it was ten minutes more than right now, and I wish I didn't have to go anymore, because then I'd have gone already and Baby Annie would be unlocking the door and Harley Barrows would already be on his way with the gardenia. I wish I never had to use the bathroom when Baby Annie is in there, but I always do. Sometimes sitting on your foot takes the need away. Mama Jewell says when she has to wait, she takes deep breaths.

But I wish I hadn't taken the Kool-Aid Hallie stole for me. I really do. Kool-Aid makes it worse.

Breathe. The problem was I forgot the diet. I was thirsty.

Breathe. Drinking it also made Hallie calmer, which is a good thing because with Mama Jewell so busy with Harley's visit to Baby Annie, Hallie is worse than ever.

There. Breathe. Today. Of all days.

■

I never told anybody, but I used to hear voices inside. After Baby Annie came, it was like somebody closed the window; I'd think I could hear something far away, but when I'd listen, I couldn't make it out anymore. Once I stopped hiding under the honey locust, I couldn't hear anything at all except my stomach growling. Some days I wonder if that's why Hallie hums, to forget the quiet. But when you hum, sooner or later you have to quit, and then the quiet is even worse.

I don't think about this much anymore, not if I can help it. It doesn't matter anymore, not to anybody. Not now that Baby Annie lives here.

■

Mama Jewell's about to come out on the porch. I can feel her mind turn to it as she takes the first batch out of the oven. The smell is fudge and it floats out the windows and doors, oily and thick. When it's strong enough, Hallie's hum shoves her off the porch and around the corner. She'll be on her hands and knees under the kitchen window, going back and forth and back in the dead petunias there. The smell of fresh fudge scares her. It's like when somebody's playing ball in the playground across the street and Tip starts whining from the porch, wanting and wanting. But Hallie can't be good, she can't hold back, not like Tip and me. The bees in her mouth start stinging if she tries. She'll have to get in the kitchen and swipe as much as she can. I know this and I know she's already sorry because Mama Jewell and Baby Annie will be so mad. But that's all she knows how to do, and she knows how thankful Tip will be. That's why she'll have to do it.

Mama Jewell's sneakers coming down the hall sound like Tip's feet with no claws. The screen door cries open. "Whatever are you doing sitting out in that sweater, Christina? It's hot enough out here to choke a horse."

I don't say boo. Mama Jewell thinks I'm backward like Hallie. She thinks I don't know what hot is or what day it is or that Baby Annie is beautiful. She thinks, like everybody else, that I sit here empty until she comes along to explain things.

"All right," she says, slapping her apron. "Be that way. Drown to death in your own perspiration." Then her voice brightens, sliding upwards. Someone must be across the street in the playground or maybe over at Sheriff Whatly's, watching. "Here you are, Christina," she says, putting a plate in my lap. "Lean over now when you eat. Use your napkin. And please don't let me catch you trying to give any to Hallorie. She's already been into the candy dish." When Mama Jewell pauses, I feel her eyes looking around the yard. "Now, I thought I told that child to stay put—"

"I don't want any," I say.

She turns to me. "But you love my fudge." She clucks her

tongue and speaks louder. "Why, from the look of it, people must think I'm some kind of monster that never feeds her children. Are you trying to starve yourself to death?"

"Baby Annie didn't eat."

"Baby Annie's on a diet. Harland likes a slim figure and we have to be—"

"Careful of complexions," I say.

Mama Jewell leans over the back of the swing so no one will hear. "What's the matter now," she says, straightening my sweater.

"Nothing."

Mama Jewell's hands stop and then disappear. "Don't sit with your leg under you like that in public. Only dogs sit that way."

The plate in my lap goes away. "Suit yourself, Miss Particular," she says loud and bright. "In any case, I made these for Harland—but honest to Betsy," she says, opening the screen door. "Sometimes you look like the Grim Reaper the way you mope. Haven't you learned to smile yet?"

"I have to pee," I say.

She stops, holding the door. "But you just went."

"That was then."

"Young lady," she says. "That was no more than fifteen minutes ago."

"It feels longer."

"Then take deep breaths," she says. "You can't keep bothering Baby Annie. She's trying to fix herself up for her young man."

As if I didn't know who her young man was or why he's coming or what he's bringing. "I did," I say.

But her mind has already gone back inside to see if the

next batch of fudge bars is done. "You did what?" she says.

"I already took deep breaths."

"Then take some more. You've got to realize that today is—"

But I can't hear the rest. With my foot not under me anymore, I have to go worse than ever. "I can go out in the garden if you want—"

"My God!" I feel her mind come rushing back to where we are. "You'll do no such thing!" she says. She leans into my face. "I am sorry," she whispers, "but if you think this is some kind of animal farm we're running, I don't mind telling you—why, my God, what would happen if Pearl was to look out her window or Harland drove by—or Oren Whatly! To see you up to such a thing! It would be dreadful, it would be . . . *appalling*, I'd lose—"

I can smell Baby Annie's lipstick. "Mama Jewell?"

"Don't you Mama Jewell me." Her voice is sharp enough to stop us both. Then she sighs, rich and smooth as fudge. "Oh, all *right*," she says. "Baby Annie's told me to keep you out of her hair and I've done my best—but you just remember, she's nervous and you're not helping." She bangs the screen behind her and starts down the hall. "And leave that mangy thing of yours outside," she calls. "I've just cleaned and I don't plan to do it again."

I take a deep breath and then another before I can stand up. Tip's harness squeaks. "Tip. Stay." I take one more deep breath, all the way down to the bottom of me until I'm not even sure I have to go anymore. Then I turn and follow the wall into the house.

When Tip isn't with me, I get "watch out for the throw rug in the hall," or "use the handrail," or "don't forget the door's shut." I tell Mama Jewell not to, because it gets me mixed up and then I go and do wrong exactly the thing she expects me to do wrong. Because then sounds don't make sense and smells don't count, and all that's left is dark and her voice and maybe the cane going tap tap. Like you're buried alive and listening to somebody trying to get through from the other side of somewhere else you don't know. That's when I make mistakes. I forget if I'm standing or sitting or walking or talking or alive or dead. Then it's darker than ever.

But today she's forgotten. Today she's worried about Harley's fudge bars. She scurries down the hall that runs through this house like a train tunnel and pushes through the swinging door to the kitchen. I go to the bathroom door and wait there for her to remember. The smell of fudge is sweet, sticky smoke. Even though she's tried to trap it in the kitchen, it's leaked out into the hall. It's like a fever in the walls, like our home is on fire. Behind me on the porch, Tip is beginning to fret.

Mama Jewell says dogs can't be sad, but Tip, he's filled fat with sadness. He can feel sad when his tail wags just like I can feel all dark and glassed-in when they tell me to smile. Why else would he go check his food dish every hour, when he knows full well it stays empty till dinner? And why else does he lie out in the middle of the street when the air is too hot to breathe? I feel him out there sometimes, his head turned away from our home, watching the playground hour after hour, panting, panting.

And why else but for sadness does he get up in the middle of the night? His harness squeaks when he sits up, and then his panting stops and he gets off my bed and goes to the head of the stairs. Sometimes he just stands there listening, but more often than not, he goes wandering. When he's finished, he'll come back. But I'll feel him watching me before he lays down his head and goes to sleep. Like he has a thought that needs finishing first. Or like he is wondering if I could ever understand or explain such a sadness to him.

"I'm sorry, but how can you think that?" cried Mama Jewell when I told her. "Why do you always have to be so morbid? Tip's got everything you need to be happy. There isn't anything else, can't you see that?"

She talked then like she meant it. But sometimes after everything is cooked and cleaned and sprayed and swept, she soaks her corns in a bowl of Epsom salts and weeps. And late at night when Baby Annie's off with Harley, we hear her talk in her sleep. "For me?" she cries and turns over. "Why it's lovely! But you shouldn't have gone to so much trouble! You really shouldn't have!" Her voice rises and falls in our dark house on those nights like a sparrow trapped up in the attic with Baby Annie's suitcases and the extra mattresses, trying to find a way out.

■

Mama Jewell says it's natural I smell things she can't, but she doesn't know all of it. To her it will only be a gardenia. To her, the only things that smell are burnt food and air fresheners and rum on Pearl Stiles' breath. She doesn't know I can smell the river in a fish or the color of the air under the honey locust or the day Baby Annie will have blood in her panties. She doesn't want to know. She wants to believe I'm blank until she fills me up, until she makes fudge for me or wears perfume.

If she could smell, she wouldn't smoke clove cigarettes when Harley comes and she wouldn't make fudge bars when it's hot out, and she'd run around the house this minute and open the windows to stir out the dark. But the only time she can smell is when Tip poops behind the couch, and then all she does about it is slap Tip, throw out the poop, and cover the sweet smell of poop over with more air freshener.

Sometimes, when Baby Annie is in the bathroom putting on smells and Mama Jewell is in the kitchen fussing with smells and it is hot and flat out like today, all the smells pile up on one another in here until you can't tell day from night or hard from soft or walls from blankets or blankets from air. All the smells of all the years and years that have been lived through in this house, that have seeped into the walls to return in the heat of an afternoon, when they swell up and bust. Like today.

Mama Jewell. Hurry up.

"I'm coming, I'm coming," she sighs. The oven door cries shut and she starts across the kitchen, but halfway over she stops. I know what's coming next. I can hear it as if it's already come and gone.

"All right. Where is the sheet of fudge bars I just took out of the oven?" Her sneakers squeal as she turns. "I'm not kidding," she warns. "Hallorie?"

She blasts through the swinging door like a train, passing by in a roar of fire and fudge smell. "Hallorie?" She goes in the parlor, looks behind the couch. "Hallorie!"

But the parlor is too quiet, too humless. She comes back, passes me again and opens the door to the cellar. "Hallorie!"

I start moaning. "Mama Jewell."

"Just a minute," she snaps, and I feel her trying to listen.

"If Baby Annie doesn't let me in right now," I say, "I have to go on the floor."

"Oh good lord, do I have to do everything around here? Can't you simply knock on the door yourself? There's nothing wrong with your hands, you know." But all the same, she's coming. She waits and taps with one finger. "Baby Annie?" she calls. "Our friend's got to piddle again. She'll just slip in and out. I promise."

"Which one is it?" says Baby Annie.

"Christina," says Mama Jewell. Her voice is soft and pink. "Do you mind horribly? These children, you know—"

"In a minute."

Mama Jewell takes my arm and pulls me to the door. "There," she whispers. "Satisfied?" She walks back to the kitchen humming "Moon River." Sometimes I think Mama Jewell is as afraid of Baby Annie as Harley is.

After the kitchen door stops swinging, I slip down the hallway. The cellar door is still open and sure enough, I can hear her. Back behind the furnace, even though she's scared of spiders, shoving everything she can into her mouth and breaking the rest into her socks and hat for us. I ease the cellar door shut, follow the wall back to the bathroom, and lean against the door. Music—Baby Annie's new transistor radio—and a clink of something in the sink.

"Baby Annie?"

"What."

"I really do this time. I have to go."

"That's what you said last time."

I lean against the door and listen to the music. I lean with all of me. "Baby Annie?" I lick the wood, rub the inside of my lips against its paint softness, almost as sweet-tasting as fudge.

"I didn't steal the fudge bars," I say. "They're for Harley, I know."

"What?" At least I think that's what she says.

"Baby Annie?" I say.

"Jesus."

"Will you let me smell the gardenia," I say. "I mean if he doesn't—"

The door opens so suddenly I'm lost in a flood of her wet dark pink smell. "What do you *want*?"

But I forget. Because she is the smell of everything and everything that is her has made me forget. I can barely breathe.

"Well?" she asks. But she's not angry, not really. She closes the door halfway so she can face the full-length mirror Mama Jewell put up for her. I can smell the heat of her curling iron through her perfume. It's burning her hair, but the bathroom is too full of smells for her to notice.

"I'm hungry," I say. "But Hallie stole all our fudge bars. I heard her in the cellar, behind the furnace. With spiders."

"Well, goody for her," says Baby Annie. "Cripes, Har's on the team diet anyhow. I told Mama already." Her voice fades into the smell of her as she opens the curling iron, hair zithering free of the metal bar. And then on top of it all— incredible—Baby Annie lights a cigarette in there, the match sound and smell and then smoke drifting out in the hall in the powdery steam of everything else.

"Me too," I say.

"You too what?" she says. Her voice has lost all of its edge now. We could be friends this way, she and I talking like this, like it was nothing at all to do. I let go of the wall and stand straighter, stand alone in the middle of the hallway.

"I'm on a diet, too," I say.

But she chokes on her cigarette and then the door swings open in a rush of air. I feel her staring with a force that could push me down. But me, I will stay where I am, I won't budge.

"You? On a *diet*?" she says. "Give me a break, kid. You don't weigh more than a mouse." She picks up the ashtray and takes a puff, watching me. Then she closes the door so she can look at the mirror again. "You're not like me. Everything I eat makes me big." I hear the curling iron click open and shut on more hair. "If Mama would quit trying to shove it down me all the time. All she wants is to watch me blow up into a barrel of lard, just like her. Well, fat chance, Mama." She pulls the curling iron free. "I'm not ever going to lose control like that."

"Baby Annie?"

"I don't want to sound mean or anything," she says, leaning around the door, "but I'm awful busy. Why don't you get lost or something? Your dog's whining for you anyhow. Hear him?" The door starts to close, and then by magic, opens. "And kid, like, I know you don't mean it, but don't call me Baby Annie anymore. The name's Annie. Just plain Annie. Okay?"

"Okay—" A woosh of air and a bang of the door that pushes me off balance again, and it's over. When Mama Jewell breezes through the swinging door again saying "you're not still bothering our Baby Annie, are you?" she finds me holding onto the baseboard.

"Well, for heaven's sake!" she cries, bending over me. "I might have knocked you to Kingdom Come, you behind the door like that. Come away from there, child."

When she tries to pull me up, I grab hold of her hands. They are wet and smell—they always do—like she just washed them in cantaloupes.

"How much am I?"

"What do you mean," she says, " 'how much are you?' "

"How much do I weigh?"

"Weigh?" she says. "Whatever do you want to know that for?"

"How much?"

"Much? Much what?" She leans back and I feel her watching. "In heaven's name—" she says. "What is the matter with you?" She puts her hand on my forehead. I can smell her teeth, she's so close. "You're shaking."

"Too much," I say. "Am I too much weight?" But the words don't make sense, I can't keep my teeth from biting them apart, and my head, even though it's not night yet, even though I'm not in my bed alone, rising like a balloon to the ceiling, bump bump bump.

"Why no, child. You don't have to worry." Her voice is careful. "You're skin and bones. Why do you think I spend all my time trying to get you to eat something?"

"Skin and bones?"

"What *is* the matter? Why Tip weighs more than you . . . now, Christina, don't do that. Look here." She gets down on her knees with a grunt. "Look at the size of your arm— here, baby—compared to mine. Can you feel the difference? You couldn't be more than 80 pounds soaking wet. You're thin as a thread, Christina. One or two pounds less and you'd be nothing at all."

"Nothing?"

But Tip is waiting at the end of the hall. Whining for me

to let him in, whining for me to come out, whining for me to remember, whining and whining and whining. And I see it then, how my life will be as straight and unchanging as this hallway itself, with me waiting at one end and Tip waiting at the other and nothing in between and all the doors shut and everybody behind them busy. Because I'm not like Baby Annie, not in a million years.

So I let Mama Jewell fuss. I let her lead me back to where Tip is whining. She pulls up my sock and unbuttons my sweater and brings me a plate of sandwiches she's made for Harley. She pats my head and sits down with a sigh of relief, and together we rock the swing.

Tip is glad I'm back. He puts his head in my lap and groans. Because Mama Jewell is still worried, she pats his head. "There now," she says. "Isn't that cute?" Me, I sit still. Sooner or later she'll remember the last batch of fudge bars I can smell burning right now, and then she'll run off to save them and leave me in peace.

"Pity Moses!" she cries. "Harland's fudge bars!" The swing lurches back on a slap of chains and she is gone, her sneakers like bugs' feet skittering up the hall.

Tip starts to lie down, but I pull him up by his harness. Inside, Mama Jewell is whying over her burnt fudge.

"Hallie," I whisper. I take a cookie and split it with him. "*Hallie*, Tip." Eager to please, Tip swallows his half in a gulp and pulls me up. To the sidewalk and around the corner, either through the cellar window or across the street to the honey locust. Because Hallie's been right all along. Hallie, who understood from the first, who doesn't care what is beautiful and what is not, Hallie who cares most of all. "Hallie, Tip. Hallie." I urge Tip until he's whining with

CORSAGE

desire, until I feel his tail beat against my leg as he tugs me down the steps, the love and sadness leaking out of him, hungry, gentled, and bleak.

FIVE

WALKING THE DOG

WALKING
THE DOG

When Tom Go set out to become a man, he carried a Rand-McNally map everywhere he went. He was a thin, embattled-looking boy with white skin and fire-red hair who ran the Sugar Beet Cafe during the day and played pinball at the Rockeroy Bar at night. Because he was shy around girls his own age, he had not yet found one to love. He believed, from the look in the eyes of the men who waited at the bar at night for Willa Moon, that he would put women altogether out of his life.

"They just hold you down," he liked to tell the group who gathered on the porch of the Sugar Beet in the afternoons to watch the cars pass. "When I leave here, I'll leave no regrets." Whether or not his listeners asked for it, Tom Go would then stand up to tick off the reasons on his fingers, one by one, talking as much to himself as to anyone else.

"I'm no good at the restaurant business, I don't like farming, I can't stand heat, I'm allergic to dust and the only other choice I've got is to just sit here and take it. That or play pinball the rest of my life. Plus, I hate it to death that nobody around here seems to remember what happens from one year to the next anymore. Which in my book," he'd say, stabbing himself hard in the chest, "adds up to getting out."

Whenever Tom Go got on the subject of travel, something lit up his heart and it was hard for him to stand still. Forgetting his shyness, he would leave the cafe and wander up and down the street, scowling at women and pouncing on any man who looked as if he had the time to listen. Frank Stiles, who had more or less looked after Tom Go since the death of his parents, said it was nothing to worry about. Walking the dog, he called it, pulling the bill of his cap down and tilting his chair back on two legs. "Just like his pap and his grandpap before him. He'll outgrow it."

Tom had never known his grandfather, and he remembered his father, Red Norman, only vaguely—a restless, formidable presence who paced the house at night in his chef's cap, referred to his wife as "that woman over there" and had almost nothing to say to his seven-year-old except "watch it, boy." Red Norman had only one desire and that was to return to a small island somewhere in the South Pacific where, as a soldier in 1942, he had been left behind briefly, sick with malaria, to await transport home. In his memory, it was an island of women who wore nothing from the waist up and intensely beautiful scenery. "See this, Stiles?" he'd say at the bar, leaning across his son's dinner plate to dip his fingers in the sugar bowl. "That's what the beach feels like. That's how white it is." Sometimes he would hold his head in his hands and his voice would crack with emotion. "What am I doing here?" he'd cry and then rising to his feet, "Stiles! I can't take it anymore. We've got to get out of here. We've just got to." But Red had died in his own cafe, suffocating on an olive caught in his throat. At the funeral, Frank had stood at the back of the church, weeping openly. Afterwards he'd followed young Tom out to the back porch and put his hand on the boy's shoulder. "Don't worry, son. I know you loved him. Maybe he was a little hard on folks like your mom, but he was searching for something. Nobody can blame a man for that." Tom had watched Frank stare out at the flats with a heave of sadness, and he had gone back in the house to help his mother lay out the food. He felt nothing over his father's death but relief. Yet nine years later, his mother buried, Frank Stiles gone to flab, and some white-hot afternoons when the dust had settled and the street was quiet and the only customers in the Sugar Beet were flies, Tom could feel the need to leave spreading through him as surely as if he were coming down with a fever.

His friends tried to help. Oren Whatly said San Diego was Tom's best bet, Jake Loper said he had heard Florida was nice, and Harley Barrows suggested he and Tom go on a spree through Mexico. Frank Stiles held out for Rock Island and even offered Tom his station wagon. But Tom felt his whole life before him and if he was ever to feel the wonder of it, there was only one solution. He had discovered it while at the arcade one Saturday in Mason City, an Arctic parka hanging in the window of an Army Navy store across the street. One sleeve was torn and the other smelled of grease, but the thing fit him like a fat glove, with wide pockets for supplies and a dog-ruff hood that closed around his face like a periscope. Looking at himself in the mirror, Tom Go felt his future before him coiled and aimed like a harpoon. "Alaska," he whispered. He bought the coat on credit, and from then on, whenever he had to drive to Mason City for supplies, as convinced of his luck as any sourdough bound for the Klondike, he stopped at the Army Navy to search the winter camping aisles.

He also always bought two dollars' worth of lottery tickets at the Discount Center. For reasons of his own, he usually kept these in his wallet until he was back home and seated again at the cafe. "I guess I'm different from most people around here," he'd say, pouncing on Sam Waters and his wife Edie when they came in for lunch after seeing Edie's doctor. "That's why I can't stay here much longer. I gotta go someplace wild where nothing's settled yet and nothing's easy. I'll just never belong here, I guess." Sam Waters would wave the boy off, but it never stopped Tom. Astride an idea with luck in his pocket, Tom Go was invincible. "I know what you're thinking. I don't know what Alaska's like, right? I don't even know what I've got to face. But that's the point. I don't know anything except that I got to try myself. It's what I'm good for." And later when he was working at the bar, he'd mutter, "Look at them," jamming another dime into the pinball machine. "Talk, talk, talk. Nobody believes anything anymore. Nobody cares."

Tom Go traced the Alkan Highway on his Rand-McNally until holes appeared in Canada. He read books about the beauty of the wilderness and what happened when a man went into it. Hypothermia, the importance of matches, the danger of sleep. "Alaska," he whispered, turning his back on his customers to scratch the silver off his lottery tickets.

Sometimes he would go home afterwards and zip himself in the parka until only his eyes showed and stand in front of the mirror, looking at himself. Once he lay down on his bed and found himself at the cafe knee-deep in snow, wielding his mop like a bat for protection while timber wolves out in the front room slithered between the tables.

Tom Go awoke in a sweat only partly caused by the parka. He got up and went to the window and looked down at the street. Then he went back to the bed and lay down again, holding an unscratched lottery ticket. To the ceiling he hissed, "Alaska." His heart was pounding.

Most people in Stygo, if they had any opinion at all, said they liked young Tom, or at least found no reason not to. Alaska didn't fool them. They knew where he would be in five or ten years. Some of them might not have known about themselves—a person can hang around a town all his life and not know about himself—but they knew about Tom. Whenever he got on the subject of leaving, they just let him talk.

There were nights at the Rockeroy, of course, when having had too much of his agreeable audience, Tom Go turned desperate. Then he would pull the bill of his cap down over his forehead and swagger back and forth at the bar demanding someone fight him. When Frank found out, he got angry. "That's enough, you little Yukon jackass," he said. "Pipe down before somebody smacks you."

But Frank was wrong. No one really minded. Tom Go's ranting was in some ways a comfort. People in Stygo worked hard for very little, and to walk in the bar at the end of the day and hear Tom Go reassuring himself of leaving, leaving, leaving, reassured those who'd come to drink that he'd be there long after they'd left.

There was only one person in town who believed Tom and that was Caroline Potts, who worked with him in the Sugar Beet Cafe. She was a lonely, efficient woman from West Bend who lived in a room over the cafe. She had an unhealthy, doughlike complexion with black undelighted eyes and hands that from the wrists down were chapped raw from being scrubbed every night with lye soap. She cooked for the Sugar Beet, but since there were few customers after the noon rush, she spent most of her afternoons next to the radio in the kitchen, lost in talk shows, which she listened to religiously. Caroline did not in the least think Tom Go was walking the dog. The day he knocked down a salesman from Mason City who was reciting all the towns he'd visited, Caroline whispered to herself, "*yes*." Nor was she dismayed the night she heard shouting and looked out her window to see Tom trying to pull free from Frank Stiles so he could throw everything he couldn't fit into one suitcase—including his mother's photo albums and his father's war medal—into the incinerator. During the breakfast rush, she heard him out at the counter, trying to make himself heard over the laughter and talk of crop yields and politics. She felt he was going through something powerful and strange, something no one understood but she.

If anyone in Stygo had known what Caroline Potts thought, they would have called her as big a fool as Tom Go. Tom Go, people said, was settling down just fine.

Tom Go didn't care what people said. He buried the earnings he didn't spend on pinball in a jar down in the arroyo east of Stygo. He kept hunting for new books at the library in Springer and stalking the Army Navy store's aisles on his trips to Mason City and scratching off his lottery tickets. On his birthday, he splurged on a hardback about survival knots and spent the afternoon locked in his room, practicing hitch knots.

Unlike Tom Go, Caroline Potts was not what folks in Stygo would call likeable. Although she was no better off than anyone else, she had an air of superiority and secrecy that put people off. Sometimes she stared as if people were nothing more than weak radio signals she would rather tune out. Other times she refused to look, clapping shut the service window and turning up her radio so that customers had to shout their orders through the shutters. Frank had warned her that no one appreciated it, but Caroline did not mind in the least. In a place like Stygo where everybody knows everybody else's business, secrets are not easy to come by. Secrets in Stygo are gold.

Caroline's secret was that she'd had a lover once, a boy from the Funtown carnival who roared into Stygo one morning in a long, dark purple car. The boy had a handsome, flushed face, but his habit of laughing at the wrong time in an excited way tended to scare off his audience. All morning he sat alone at the counter with his untouched breakfast, talking and laughing to himself, and when Lizzy Loper and her girlfriend Baby Annie came in at lunchtime he tried to persuade one of them to go for a drive with him. He left in a rage when neither would, saying he hated the smell of small towns and slamming the door behind him; but that night she saw his car across the street at the bar and after the bar closed, he returned to the cafe and knocked on the door until Caroline came down in her bathrobe and let him in. In the darkened front room, the boy had pulled her towards him and whispered things in her ear. Some of them were dark and frightening, but some were wonderful and strange. At one point, he embraced her, crying honey, honey, honey, as if he couldn't bear the intensity of having chosen life.

Afterwards, it seemed to Caroline that the rest of the world was full of meaningless people saying words. She put away her radio and bought a suitcase and at night she put cream on her hands to make them less red. But her lover did not return for her, and she did not get any letters, and one morning, when she accidentally overheard Sarah Zambini and the sheriff's wife gossiping at the counter, and realized suddenly that the young woman they were discussing with such ferver, Willa Moon, had left town months before on the same night her lover had, Caroline stopped waiting. She was still fairly young, but something about her had changed. People began to think of her as an old maid. At night, she sometimes left the cafe in a rage and walked out to the fields away from where people would see her, weeping and pulling up the beets, praying for something to change her life, or take it away.

But one night just before dawn when she returned to the cafe exhausted and dirty and emptied of everything but the need for sleep, she heard Tom Go out in the front room. He was standing alone by the front window and talking aloud to himself, waving his hands as if he were trying to explain himself to someone else in the room, someone he did not know very well. Caroline watched from behind the shutters of the service window, and so deep was her sudden conviction that her whole body shook. "I'll help him get out of here," she said to herself. She clenched her fists and her black eyes glowed. "I won't let him grow ordinary and dull with the rest of them."

On the surface, nothing changed. When Caroline and Tom Go were together in the bar, they treated each other like members of different species. She knew nothing of small talk, and since Tom Go didn't either, hours went by in which they did not speak at all. Still, on slow afternoons when the cafe was empty, the few words that passed between them began to take on an airy weight and substance, like spoons in a drawer being rattled by ghosts. After mopping, he might call out, "The floor's wet, so watch it," and though he expected no answer, the silence had so many things going on in it that he could not always be sure what he was thinking and what he was saying out loud. Likewise, Caroline might appear at the window to say "the mop's here," and though Tom would take it from her and do his job, his ears would burn with the mop's here, the mop's here, while she sat forgotten in the kitchen, moving the radio antenna back and forth, trying to catch something new.

Then one morning in July, a morning like any other, Tom Go drove Frank's station wagon to Mason City for supplies, spent his usual hour at the Army Navy, his usual two dollars on the lottery and another four dollars at the arcade, and found when he got back to the cafe and made himself lunch that he was holding a winning lottery ticket.

The people of Stygo were stunned. Some were incredulous, others speechless, and many, many were angry. Frank Stiles, who had bought lottery tickets twice a week for ten years, leaned forward, choked on his coffee, and laughed until tears ran down his cheeks. Here was a boy, a perfect fool of a boy, getting twenty-five hundred dollars. People threw down their tools, went to the cafe and ordered Tom Go to buy all of them lunch. The fields emptied out and within an hour the place was full. Billy Quail pulled up outside in the station wagon with his feeble-minded daughter, Kwami, and sold Red Spot from a keg on the tailgate. People were shouting, arguing, making speeches and hauling the boy back and forth between them. Everyone felt it his duty in one way or another to look after the boy, to see that he appreciate his luck properly and spend it wisely.

When Caroline heard the news, she had the urge to run out in the street shouting with joy, to make everyone understand that it was she who had known this would happen, she who understood desire, she who had believed in the power of Tom's yearning. But when she saw the crowd yelling and laughing and slapping Tom Go and each other on the back as if they all shared a natural and easy understanding, her heart narrowed. "No one would understand," she thought bitterly. "Not even the boy." She turned on the radio, re-tied her apron and took up her work. When she heard Frank come in with a case of Cold Duck, she snapped shut the service window.

"Life of the party," said Liz Loper to her husband as they leaned on each other watching the closed shutters. "Has to make them little salads just perfect."

It angered Tom Go, too. "Who does she think she is?" he yelled to Frank. "This doesn't just happen, you know." He punched open the door to the kitchen, not even pausing at the threshold. She turned to look at him, her forehead shiny from grease and sweat. He had his legs spread and he was breathing hard, his shirt wet and yanked open to the waist, his hair sticking out at an odd angle. His mouth was curled in a sneer of contempt, but when she looked in his eyes she saw that he was as frightened and helpless as something kept too long in a box. Caroline felt her throat close in anger. What Tom Go was doing was nothing less than a rehearsal, terrible in its vividness, of her own life. Years ago she had stopped waiting for her own life to begin, but she had never wanted to stop feeling the loss. She looked at Tom now and her little eyes grew hard. "I would like to know one thing," she said, "If you're so sure you're still getting out of here, why is it you're not gone?"

The color drained from Tom's face. "What do you mean?" he cried. "I only just won the ticket this morning. I haven't even cashed it." He stared at her back, his mouth opening and closing. "You mean when? I'll tell you when." He ran his hands across the top of his head. "I've got to figure things out first. It's all come at once. I mean, I've lived here all my life. I can't just leave, bang, like that. I have to think it out a little—"

Carolyn looked at him and turned back to the grill.

"For hell," he said. "Don't I have a right to enjoy myself for one night, just one night in this stupid town?"

"Would you care to know what I think?" She put down her spatula and faced him, her voice shaking. "I think you're wishing you'd never bought a lottery ticket in your whole life, or even heard the word Alaska. I think you're keeping your mouth shut now about leaving so everybody will forget that's what you wanted. Not that they won't." She turned away so he would not see her face. "Am I right, Tom Go?"

For a moment, Tom could not speak. "What do you know?" he cried at last. "You never left anywhere. You think I don't want to leave here?" and stumbling, he turned and fled back to the celebration, shouting at his neighbors to listen.

Oren Whatly and Frank Stiles decided it was best to take the boy in the squad car to cash in his lottery ticket. They stopped at the truck stop in Sweetwater, Oren's siren wa-wahing and lights flashing, to pick up Frank's older brother, Jack, who had not heard the news but was already drunk for his own reasons, and then drove on to Mason City.

While Tom Go was across the street at the Greyhound bus

station, Frank and Jack started arguing about the pros and cons of investing in land or an IRA account. They were at the point of exchanging blows when Tom reappeared holding up a ticket to Fairbanks via Edmonton. "Horse's ass," shouted Frank at Jack, pushing Tom out of the way. "The boy needs a future, not a pile of dirt," and Jack shouted back, "That's what you're saying? My whole life is dirt?" When Tom and Billy finally maneuvered them back into the car, Frank and Jack sat at opposite windows and would not speak to each other. They stopped for dinner in Clear Lake— "screw Caroline's food," said Frank, "we have that every night"—and in Algona, where Frank and Jack buried the hatchet, they stopped for a case of champagne. By the time they got back to Stygo, it was dark and in the back seat, Frank and Jack had their arms hooked around each other's neck, singing "My Old Gal." The party had moved over to the bar, people pushing and dancing out on the porch. Frank and Jack went in and Billy followed with the champagne. Tom Go stayed back to take a leak. He should have been reeling drunk, but he was not. The night sky was clear and full of stars. A dog came by, thin as bone, sniffing at tires. Tom looked at it and then at the light coming from the window of the bar. He touched the ticket in his breast pocket and turned away, feeling as lonesome and sober as he had ever felt in his life.

He could not sleep. By 5:00 A.M. he was packed, bathed, combed and dressed. He had piled all his summer clothes, which he would never need again, on top of his dresser, along with an extensive note, for Mrs. Barrows, his landlady. After tiptoeing down the hall to the bathroom, he went back to his room to strip his bed. His bus was not due to leave until noon. He sat in the chair by the window, his suitcase on the floor next to his parka. At 6:35, when he spotted Kwami Quail, squatting in the shadows of the alley across the street and staring up at his window, he rose angrily, yanked down the shade and placed his suitcase and parka by the door. Then he went to his bed and lay down, fully dressed, and fell asleep.

By 8:00, he was awake again, pacing his room, peeking around the shade to see down the street. It irked him that no one had offered to see him off. No one the night before had even bothered saying good-bye except Willa Moon, and she'd been so drunk he doubted that she even remembered where he was going. At 8:45, when he looked out and saw that Kwami had disappeared, he decided to walk over to the bar. Show Frank and anyone else dropping in for a hair of the dog just how serious he was. He put on his cap, moved his suitcase and parka out into the hallway and after a final look around, closed the door, locking it behind him. "Adios, garbage can."

Harley Barrows was outside underneath his Camaro. After explaining that he was leaving, Tom Go left his room key on the hood of the car for Harley's mother. "You're smart to keep away from girls," called Harley from under the Camaro. "I went over to Mama Jewell's last night after the party to sneak Baby Annie out and she wouldn't even come to her window for me this time. I swear. Like I don't have a right to celebrate with my friends once in a while." He wiggled out from under the Camaro and looked up at Tom. "Why are women like that, I wonder?"

"I don't know, I guess." Tom looked down the street. In his coat and tie, he was uncomfortably aware of not being a part of things anymore. "So long, Har."

He was halfway down the street before he realized he'd left the bus ticket and the money on the bureau in his room. He dropped his suitcase and parka and ran all the way back to the boarding house. To his relief, Harley was still there. Tom took the key and ran upstairs for the money and the ticket. When he returned, he handed Harley the key again and shook his hand this time. "Well, this is it," he said. After a moment in which they were both a little confused, Harley held up a coupling. "You don't know nothing about universal joints on Camaros, do you?"

Tom ran his hands through his hair. "I'll write you a letter if I can when I get there. Maybe you can drive up. Bet you'd like it. Baby Annie, too."

"Nah. Baby doesn't like shit."

"Maybe just you, then. Why not, huh? Forget Mexico."

"Yeah, why not?" But when Tom looked back, Harley was already under the car again.

The street was deserted. As he walked, Tom Go leaned forward, angry at the whole town now, his eyes screwed to slits. "Assholes," he muttered when he saw no one waiting on the porch in front of the Rockeroy. "Can't even get out of bed for me." He went over to the cafe and let himself in, propping the door open behind him.

The front room still held the smells of the night before. Light coming through the front window turned the air a thick, sleepy gold. Tom Go listened and for a moment had the feeling that everyone in the world except him and maybe Kwami Quail had somehow left Stygo. But then he realized it was Sunday. Caroline would not be down until noon. Frank and the others were at church.

By the clock over the cash register, he had another hour before church let out. He put his parka in one of the booths and loosened his tie. He might just as well mop the floor as stand there. Certainly it would not get done until Caroline found someone to take his place. This cheered him considerably. "One last time," he said, "and then, old pal—" He hefted his suitcase into the booth, took off his jacket and went around the room putting the chairs up on tables.

In the kitchen, while he waited for the pail to fill, he felt as if he were seeing details he had never seen before. The beige paint his father had coated the kitchen with, the veil of dust on the fan, the grease stain above the stove, Caroline's fingerprints on the shutters of the service window. Remembering Caroline made him mad all over again. He turned on the radio, switching from her Dr. Sam show over to Country Western. "Old maid." When the pail was full, he turned off the water, got the mop from behind the door and went out to the front room.

He worked quickly in widening circles, his mind a blank, the thick slap and suck of the string mop against wood. He felt a certain satisfaction as he worked. He did the counter area and the restrooms and ended up at the door to the kitchen again, perspiring heavily.

By the clock, Frank and the others would be leaving church. Whistling, Tom Go went out the back door to dump the dirty water over the fence. On the way to the kitchen he stopped in the pantry for floor wax.

But behind him a radio announcer was repeating the number if you wanted to talk to Dr. Sam. Tom's heart sank. He had said good-bye to her the day before. At the urging and applause of everyone in the cafe, he had even kissed her cheek when he handed her the keys. Now he'd have to go through with it again. He did not look around, but crossed the kitchen, shoved the pail under the faucet and slapped on the water taps.

On this day, however, Frank—who had been too hungover for church—happened to be next door washing the dust off his truck. When Tom Go turned on the tap he found there was no water pressure.

For several minutes he stood there, rigid, while the water tinkled merrily into the pail. Who did she think she was anyway? Why couldn't she just let him go? Tom Go closed his eyes. He wouldn't have to take this tomorrow, or the day after, or the day after that. He would never have to deal with her again. This was the last time. He stared into the pail and realized that he didn't have to take it now. He could leave, he could just walk out the door. It would make no difference because after today, he was never coming back. He would never have to stand there feeling awkward and ashamed of himself again. "Tell me when it's full," he said and rushed out the swinging door to the front room.

But he had forgotten the floor was still wet. With a crash he went down, whacking his head on the edge of the coffee machine.

He was on his back looking up. The end of one of the long fluorescent ceiling tubes was covered with spider sacks and cobwebs. He blinked several times. Caroline Potts was beside him. She looked frightened. She held up her hand in front of his face and wiggled her fingers. It was as if she were waving good-bye to him, as if they were in a train station, as if she were someplace on the other side of a pane of glass. Her face came closer until it was inches away. When it tilted from one side to the other, he realized that she was not lonely or plain-looking after all, but only unhappy. It seemed to him a terrible thing to realize this as something he had not known before. He thought about Alaska, about himself and how he would feel having left home after all his talk of it, and his throat tightened in self-pity. Because he did not want her to see him cry, he closed his eyes. Oh honey, she cried, honey, honey, but because she was rocking him against her breasts, he did not just yet want to look.

S I X

WHAT LASTS

WHAT LASTS

Mr. Berard likes our new mailbox. He's lived out here all his life and he found my mother the last time she got lost in the corn, and he told Pop a high mailbox is a damn good idea because otherwise, come July, no one will be able to find anybody. That's how deep the corn grows around our place and how far out in the middle of it we are. It's a mile long and a mile wide and it's all corn and sky and along the edge of it, where Route 34 runs, about one car a day. You can stand out in the middle of a hot day and forget your own name. You can forget what direction you're facing or what direction you came from or how long you've been gone. Corn, corn, corn. Maybe in town, where there are houses and clocks and dates to remember, forgetting where you are is a sign of something, like Mama Jewell said. But out here, forgetting doesn't mean squat. Forgetting is easy. If you never lived out in the middle of it like we do, you can't know.

That's why Pop built the mailbox. Our other mailboxes were the regular kind, like Mama Jewell has in town. Three of them ended up shot to death and lying in the ditch with their jaws kicked in, and the fourth one I found out in the corn up at the north end, squashed so flat and full of bullet holes I wasn't even sure whose it was, it looked so different.

But not this one. This one's got an iron leg six feet tall planted in concrete and it's big as a steamer trunk. Quarter-inch steel Pop and I painted pitch black, WATERS: RT 34, it says, arc-welded, drilled, and riveted, right out there on the highway next to our front gate, pointing out who we are and where we live. It's got a jaw as big as a serving dish and a silver flag on top as long as Pop's arm. Mr. Berard crisscrosses the whole county to deliver mail and he says there's nothing like our mailbox anywhere except here. It's so tall he has to get out of his car to toss mail in, and I have to stand on the top rail of our front gate to fish it out. But nobody's going to run this one over, and nobody's going to miss it either. If you ever got lost, like my mother did last time, even if you headed east where there are miles to go, miles before you find anything but corn, still there will be the mailbox when you're ready to come home. Mama Jewell and the sheriff, Mr. Whatly, and the others in town, they can talk what they want about Pop's new ideas. They'll drive past our place and just like my mother when she goes on her walks, they'll know it a mile off.

It's early afternoon, and Pop and I are finishing with George Washington, our prize hog, when she comes out on the porch. She's got her hair pulled back with barrettes, she's holding her pocketbook, and she's wearing Pop's muck boots again. I drop the hog pole on the steps and slip back down into the root cellar, calling into the dark. Pop's on a kitchen chair in the back, his head sinking over a carton of seasonings in his lap, his feet tucked pigeon-toed under the chair, the flashlight still in his hand. Nowadays he is always tired. I pull his hair and shout Pop! and he staggers to his feet, dropping the carton. Edie, he calls and thunders up the steps out into the yard, hog knives dangling like teeth from his belt. I put the spices back in the box and the box back on the shelf, and he is already beside her, I can hear him out there in the dusty heat, telling her about falling asleep while looking for hog salt, poking fun at himself. "Oh Sam," she says, and I hear her laugh. My mother has a nice clean laugh. Through the shaft of light from the door I can see the edge of the smokehouse roof and the gray smoke of George Washington curling around it and all the rest of the sky that hangs over our fields, waiting to take it in.

"That's some mailbox, isn't it?" Pop is saying when I come out. His voice is still heavy with sleep. He is cupping her elbow in one hand and fumbling to pull up his suspenders. "You could see it from here to Mason City," he says. He finishes with his suspenders and slides his hand down her arm to her wrist before letting go. "Couldn't you, Edie?"

"My goodness," gasps my mother, laughing for us. "You certainly can." She opens her pocketbook and begins to hunt through it, pawing loose change from one side to the other. "Does anybody here know what time it is?"

Pop's eyes are on the mailbox, his face tight with satisfaction. I take her arm, so skinny nowadays that her wrist feels like a piece of corn shuck wrapped around bone, and I point to the cracked face of her watch. "Look," I say. "Ten to five."

"Ten to five," says my mother. "Oh my."

"You remember how I used to get us lost up in Wyoming, Ead?" says Pop. "We didn't have a landmark to look for in those days, did we. I remember one time we were out till dawn." He turns to me. "Your grandma Maple was ready to shoot me when I brought her back."

"You were awful," says my mother suddenly. "You told

me we were heading east and we headed straight for the reservoir. You told Mother we had a flat."

"A flat," says Pop in delight. "I did say we had a flat. I did. How in the heck did you remember that, Ead?"

My mother stops. She puts her hand on her chest like she is catching her breath. "Well," she says, looking young and flushed. "I don't quite know."

"But you remember the reservoir?" says Pop pressing at her. "Palmer reservoir? You remember the flat?"

"Oh god," she says, waving him off to open her pocket-book. "Who could forget?"

Pop turns to the view, his whole face lighter. "Ead," he says. "You're getting better now. Every day a little better. I'm sure of it."

"Of course it is," says my mother. But she's not listening. I hold up her wrist to show her her watch again. Pop's hand comes down between us.

"Not now, Ruth," he says. "If she wants to go for a walk, she goes for a walk."

My mother covers her mouth and looks at Pop. "Is Oren coming today or is it tomorrow? I have to make dinner now, don't I? Isn't it time?"

"Actually," says Pop, checking his watch, "It's almost one. Three minutes to one to be exact. And besides, Ruth and I are making dinner. Barbecue tonight, via George Washington. Fatback ribs, just the way you like them. We've been working all day on him. We have it all under control."

My mother looks frightened. "But what if that woman Jewell Peske shows up with him?" she says. "What if she doesn't like barbecues?"

"Mama Jewell can't come," I say. "Pop told her not to.

She's not allowed. Neither is Mr. Whatly or Dr. Seymour. Remember?"

"Aaa—" Pop breathes in and slaps his chest. "If I were you, Ead, I'd take a walk. Relax. Get some of this clean healthy air in your lungs."

My mother stands there. She looks at Pop and then closes her mouth and looks at me.

"She doesn't have to go for a walk," I say, "does she?"

Pop talks at me with his eyes and then he looks away.

"But Pop," I say. "She's got on the muck boots. Where's she going to go with muck boots?"

"That's enough," he barks.

My mother flattens her dress against her legs to look, and the way she does it, the thing that stops behind her eyes when she sees her feet, makes my stomach skip. "Oh no," she says. She pushes the strap of her pocketbook up to the crook of her elbow and puts her hand over her mouth. When she bends for a closer look, the points of her spine rise up sharp enough to tear through her dress. I want to touch her, but Pop is there, watching.

"Ruth," he says. "Why don't you go marinate the meat for us."

"They're all wrong," says my mother. "Aren't they." She straightens up and stares at Pop. "They're too black, Sam," she says. "They're much too black. My slippers are better than these."

"Okay, slippers." His voice is getting tighter. "Don't go for a walk then. You put the boots on, take them off. You can do that, can't you?"

"Of course I can do that," says my mother, her voice rising. "But these are much too black. These aren't right at all."

"No," cries Pop. "They're wrong. You're right. They're totally wrong. Go." He turns and slams open the screen door. "Slippers are a damn good idea."

My mother rolls her eyes and then looks over at me and moves her mouth. "It's ten to five," I say.

My mother sighs with relief. She turns to Pop. "So there," she says, and goes back inside, clomping across the kitchen floor back to her bedroom.

I look at Pop but he will not look.

"She was going to leave," I whisper. "I saw the way she came out the door. She had her pocketbook and those boots, just like before—"

Pop leans into my face. "Who do you think you are," he asks. "Some kind of mind reader? I should knock you straight into next week." But instead, he lifts back and waves his arms. "Maybe she wanted to wear muck boots for a change. Maybe her feet are cold. Maybe she thought it would rain. God almighty," he says, turning to me, "what business is it of yours what she thinks?"

"It's not my business," I say, edging away. "You were asleep."

"And that gives you the right to tell her she's wrong?"

"You do."

"Yeah?" he says and then he roars, "Well, I'm not thirteen years old neither."

My mother is coming back, the big black boots shuffling across the linoleum. Pop gives me a last look and pulls away. Sometimes he is like a rifle about to fire, his face nearly purple with it. He puts his hands on his hips to stop it and stares out at the view.

My mother is behind the screen door with a grocery bag

in her arms, pushing against the hinged side. "Here," I say, stepping back. "This way."

"Well," she says when I open the door. "So there you are."

"I'm hungry." I step around her. "Anybody want lunch?" But by the time I get back, it's too late. She is already out to the edge of the corn. Pop is watching from the porch, his hands hanging at his sides now like things that do not belong to him. "No," he says hoarsely when I try to slip past. "She's going for a walk." He clears his throat and calls out to her.

"No more getting lost then," he says, licking the edge of his mouth. "How 'bout it, Ead?"

But my mother does not answer. She walks quickly, in spite of the boots, leaning forward over the bag like the wind is blowing, like she is late for something, like she has heard someone calling for her out in the corn.

■

Three hours later, I'm on the porch, mixing potato salad and listening to the blackbirds call good night. Pop is wolfing down half a jelly sandwich and keeping his eyes on the distance. The sky is beginning to cool at the edges, but there's no movement in the dark green wall of corn around the house, nothing but heat ghosts rising from the fields. No problem, says Pop, she'll be hungry soon, she'll smell dinner cooking, but when the grill is ready, instead of sending me to the kitchen for the ribs, he sends me up in the silo for a bird's eye.

From the top window I watch Pop walking around the yard, calling, his shadow a black crowbar following his feet. Over in the side yard, the coals in the barbecue look like a little piece of sunset fell out of the sky. For every direction the corn is still. Route 34 is empty. I wiggle onto the sill and pull my half of the jelly sandwich out of my shirt. I take a bite and put it down to pick at a spot on my shorts. It could be that Mama Jewell and Sheriff Whatly have come back and picked her up on the road. Maybe she had clothes in the bag she was carrying. Maybe they're taking her to Mason City. There are lots worse things that could happen. What if the ladder broke and I had to stay up here all night? What if I fell, scratching my nails against the metal siding all the way to the bottom? The echo would turn me deaf before I died. What if they all died? But when I look between my feet and see how dark it's gotten down below all at once, so that even Pop has disappeared now, I get a shiver so bad my teeth knock. I scat down and run home, feeling my way through the corn.

The way he's slamming around the house, turning on lights, calling, calling, I know it's for real this time. Mama Jewell and Mr. Whatly have scared him. "Get out of the way dammit," when I bump into his heels. Attic, pantry, closets, mud room. She's taken her slippers, she's taken her Air Force parka. I start calling too. Over the black corn the moon is coming now, round as an orange. Pop walks to the barn without bending his legs. Tool shed, stalls, smokehouse, the station wagon, even George Washington's butcher pen. Pop stops me in the hayloft. "Now wait a minute," he says. He sits on a bale and holds my shoulder. By the bare bulb light, his face glitters pale under straw dust and sweat. "There's no need to lose our heads. What we need is perspective." Pop believes in perspective. He looks at me. "Lighten up, part- ner. Edie probably just wanted a little peace and quiet." He gets up to re-stack the bales and sits again, making me sit, too, resting a hand on my knee. "Now then," he says, wip- ing his face. "Now we put on our thinking caps."

His eyes go away, like he's forgotten everything, even me. When I can't stand it any longer, I get up and head-butt him. His belly gives like a pillow. "What," he says. "You think I'm giving up? No faith, that's your problem. I know her. She's got on that fancy dress of hers, she's not going to try cross-ing the fence this time. What we do is go to the south end and work our way around from opposite directions until we meet at the mailbo—" He and I look at each other, shocked, and then I'm on the ladder. "Slow down," he shouts, "you'll break your damn neck," but as I run out across the yard lit up like a stage in the moonlight, and break into the dark corn, I can hear stalks already snapping behind me and, in a stride, he's pushed me out of the way and gone on ahead. "Edie! Edie!" The moon shines on his bald spot. I follow with my hands up, stumbling blind over the rows.

She's at the foot of the mailbox, sitting on the cinder-blocks with the parka on. When we come busting through the corn, she stands up, scared by our noise. She's holding something in both hands and the moon shining on Route 34 behind her is so bright I can see her legs through her dress, two pale sticks coming out from the bulk of her parka and disappearing into the big black muck boots.

"Is the phone for me?" she says.

"Wait—" Pop is sweaty and wheezing for breath. He holds up one hand and leans over to catch his wind. "Shit, Edie," he says. "I haven't run—like that—since I was—in the army. You must be—trying to kill me." He leans back to say something else, but when he sees what she's holding, he stops dead.

"Mom," I say. "What are you doing with George Wash-ington's ribs?"

I don't mean it to be funny, but Pop is laughing. He bunches up his shoulders and points at the pan of ribs and then at me and then he rocks forward, slapping his legs. When he rears back, the gold filling in the back of his mouth glints at the moon. He's got tears on his cheeks, he's shaking and helpless with it, holding his sides and bowing over. "Oh," he says. "Oh. Oh."

My mother looks thin and shivery as paper. She looks down at that plate of barbecue as if she doesn't know what it's doing there in her hand, and she hands it to me.

"Pop," I say. "Come on. It's not funny."

"Didn't the phone ring?" she says. "I thought I heard the phone."

My voice feels like something crawling out of itself, crawling over Pop's laughter and off into the corn. "The phone?" I say. "We don't have a phone anymore. Pop threw it away. We don't have one anymore." I turn to Pop and stamp my foot. He has his back to us, he's shaking his head at the moon with his hands on his hips. "Pop, you stop laughing. You've got to quit it now."

"Sam," she says and the way she says it, so sharp and clear all of a sudden, makes Pop freeze. "This is so ridiculous," she says. "I think something is wrong with me."

"Wrong?" says Pop, turning. His voice is furry. "Wrong with you?"

"Well yes," she says sharply. "Of course there is."

"Edie," Pop sighs and wipes his face. "You found the mailbox, didn't you?"

"But I've been looking for hours and I can't find a single other familiar thing," she says. Her voice is rising on itself. "I can't even find my house. What is all this corn?"

Pop stares at her a moment and then he turns to me. "Go home," he says. "Get."

But I don't. "Mom," I say. "Mom, it's ten to five."

My mother isn't listening. There is something inside her that is not her anymore, it has been there for a long time but now I can see it pushing both her eyes out. It is breathing through her mouth, pushing her aside to listen through her ears, and nothing Pop and I have done can stop it. My mother points at the mailbox, her finger as pale and thin as corn stubbles. "This is not my mailbox," she says.

"Oh Edie," says Pop. He takes a step closer and she raises her hand to strike. "No," he says. "Edie, it's me. I'm your husband." He reaches for her slowly. She is staring out at the world like something with its foot caught in a trap. He unpins the barrette that is dangling by her cheek and re-fastens it to the top of her head. "Sometimes everybody's crazy," he says to her. "Sometimes nobody's right anymore."

I haven't said anything, I haven't breathed, but he turns and looks fiercely at me then like I have. "You don't believe me?" he says. "You don't think I'm right?" With one hand, he picks up the pan of George Washington's ribs. "Then watch," he says and throws them, pan and all, into the corn.

My mother is crying, holding the furry hood of the Air Force parka against her cheeks. Pop puts his arm around her and she leans into him as if blown by wind and I watch them go down the driveway, fading into the dark towards the house in the corn. They are one shadow with two arms and four legs and then they are nothing at all.

The quiet out on Route 34 shines off in either direction, bright as a rope of silver. After a while, I step up on the gate and pull down the jaw of the mailbox. It drops like the mouth of a furnace. There is nothing inside but the dark and a bullet hole in the very back, a sting of moon shining through.

I push off from the gate and wedge inside. I wiggle in to my waist until my shoulders are pinned. Behind me, where I can't see, I feel a little breeze brush the back of my legs.

Maybe I'll get stuck trying to get out and Pop won't come. Maybe someone driving along Route 34 for a potshot won't notice my legs sticking out. Lots of things could happen. Worse things than this.

I find the spent bullet and pick it up with my teeth. I roll it around on my tongue and I swallow it, bitter and real.

But the mailbox will last. Maybe Pop won't and neither will my mother, but the mailbox will. It will last with or without us. It will last forever. And when I square my eye to the pinhole, I see our old house at the end of time, with everyone gone and all the windows and doors blown out and the corn growing wild and up to the windows, twisting and tangling and reaching inside.

SEVEN

CALLIOPE

CALLIOPE

 Shortly after my brother was arrested up in North Dakota, Mother disowned him. It was not that she didn't love him—I think she would have sacrificed everything we had if it would have gotten Mick anywhere—but after we learned what he'd done to the Winkers, loyalty was out of the question. A mixed-up older brother is one thing, a psychopath is another. We'd had all we could take. Which is why I'm not going to tell you much about him. You want his story, read that book Hermann Delp wrote. You probably already have. All I want to say is that because of Mick, the FBI had our car, the store in Stygo took back our credit, we had to change churches, and lawyers from as far away as Chicago were offering to prosecute Mick for free. We had writers calling to offer us money for what we remembered, and souvenir hunters pawing through our garbage at night. Sometimes people from Stygo drove all the way out to our house just to tape magazine pictures to our front door of what Mick had done. They wanted to know if we could love him now, if we had ever loved him, if we could understand. Disownment was the only way.

I was almost seventeen at the time, a fact I record not for the sake of sympathy but because it is one way of explaining why I, for one, was glad to be rid of my brother. One or two

years younger and I might still have been a fool for him, the way my sister, Mary, was; any older, and I might have tried to outdo him myself. But I was the middle child, the sensible one Mother never worried about, and although I had sat in on all the discussions about Mick—Mick's future, Mick's intelligence, Mick's insomnia, Mick's ambitions, Mick, Mick, Mick and how all his plans were going to tie up with ours—I was just as glad when it was over and we could stop fooling ourselves. There was no hope for Mick. When it came to responsibility, Mick was lost. Guilt only made him worse. Always restless and itchy and hungry to fight, always telling us what he was going to do and then slamming doors and staring out the window, hating us for not letting him do it, for needing him to look after us, for expecting him to stay. As far as I could see, what he had done to the Winker family was nothing more than the culmination of everything he had ever dreamt of doing to Mother and Mary and me.

Still, letting go was not easy. Mick's wildness had become a way of life. After he was gone, there was nothing to do. Not that I minded. It was just that Funtown was so suddenly quiet. The quiet of a root cellar after a twister has passed over. The quiet of an empty room after someone slams the door. Mother dealt with it by cleaning. She cleaned everything—not just the floors and windows and walls and furniture, but the coils on the back of the refrigerator, the inside of the air conditioner casing, the innards of the chromed tubes that made up the legs of our kitchen table and chairs. At night when she couldn't sleep she scraped between the linoleum tiles on the floor in the kitchen with a paring knife. But she was all right. As upset as she was to lose Mick, you could tell she was not much surprised. Maybe she'd even expected it. I certainly had. In any case, now that facts had to be faced, she was cutting her losses and making do, as she always had, with what we had left.

But my sister I was worried about. Mary was only fourteen and because of a fierceness in her nature which at times had made her almost as impossible to cope with as Mick, all she had ever talked about was him. She had believed that he was the brother she wanted, that they were kindred spirits, that the reason he couldn't get along with Mother and me and everyone else in Funtown was because he was aiming for something better. Always chasing after him to tell him he was right, always defending him when he left her behind, always bragging about him with that ferocious gleam in her eye, challenging me or anyone else to file a complaint. Even when we heard he'd taken that girl, Willa Moon, with him for luck, even then Mary said he was right. But since the day the FBI men had proved that the blood stains on a pair of Mick's pants he'd hidden under the bed were human, Mary had not even spoken his name. She could talk about other things now—who she liked, who she didn't like, who she thought might be an ally at school, what job she wanted next summer, what clothes she wished she could buy, which classes she hated enough to fail—but not about Mick. Those days were over. She could not talk about him anymore. The night after we heard he'd been sentenced, as she and I lay in bed listening to Mother crying out in the kitchen, I felt something moving in the back of Mary's mind, loosening the ropes in the dark, pulling at her blood and beginning to whisper. But I whispered back. "Shut up, you idiot. It's too late. Go to sleep." And after a long time, she did.

I grew up that winter. I settled down. Mother depended on me for it and so did Mary. I took back the travel books Mick had stolen for me from the library in Mason City. I started making the bed and doing dishes. It wasn't so bad. I got along. I didn't need to remember Mick. I suppose the peace and quiet got to me a little—in winter when the fair is gone and the blizzards go on for weeks at a time, Funtown is not much more than a parking lot out in the sagebrush with a circle of trailers in the middle, all strapped down to keep them from blowing away. But after *Newsweek* came out with "Who is to Blame?" which included not only pictures of Mick in jail but earlier pictures of him at home, laughing, with his arms around Mother and Mary and me—pictures which Hermann Delp stole from Mother's album the night he invited himself to dinner—the Funtown I thought I'd hated was not such a bad place to be. It was certainly a better place than trying for a new start in Stygo, or anywhere else for that matter, anywhere in America where people read *Newsweek*. In Funtown our neighbors didn't care about headlines. Most of them had troubles of their own. They didn't blame us. They knew there was no one to blame. After Mother announced we'd disowned him, no one ever talked about him again. And all that empty space for yourself when you went outside, all that clear, hard light that was always changing, that sagebrush always moving and talking to you, even when it was covered with snow and the wind in every direction. A power that buzzed in your ears, that entered your brain and made you want to shout. Step out in the middle of it and you forgot why your brother was gone or why no one but your sister would sit next to you on the school bus. You had all the rest of it to take you in. No, I didn't mind the quiet. Mother was probably expecting me to be interested in boys or books, but if bad weather closed the highway, I was just as glad to stay home. And by February when *Life* magazine knocked on our door for an exclusive on Mick and why at nineteen he had managed to end up on death row, even Mary, who hated to agree with me on anything, was ready to give in. Who wanted the outside world anymore? Who needed it? If anything, Mick had done us a favor. He had made us appreciate Funtown.

In spring, the quiet went away. The carnival-ride semis were rumbling into Funtown for the summer, and despite Mother's new Electrolux, our trailer was full of dust. Mary and I had one week to ourselves, and we spent most of it in the midway, talking over the yeowl and slur of the calliope to the summer help Fun Harrison brought in for the fair. Some were locals from Stygo and those we avoided; but most of Fun's crew were overlanders—men with no past, gentle and hollow-eyed, eager to please. With them we were rough and friendly, showing them the ropes, giving advice, pretending to be older than we were, pretending to know everything, pretending to be someone else. And in many ways we were. What Mick had tried to break apart, the winter had mended. Mary and I were a pair now, the two of us different from everyone else, but the same. It turned out that if I liked someone, Mary liked him too. If I was angry at someone, he made two enemies. It was new for both of us. In some ways I think it was as close as we ever came to being friends.

But that was our vacation. Through May, June, and July we worked in six-hour day shifts. Mother worked the Three-A-Shot next to the calliope and Mary and I sold ride tickets out in the parking lot. Our booth was a little white-washed house on wheels with an orange roof and two narrow-barred windows facing out either direction. The job was bearable because the calliope wasn't close enough to ruin your hearing, but there were drawbacks. The parking lot was the hottest, dustiest place in all of Funtown. Because we handled cash, Fun had to lock us in the booth at the beginning of each shift and pass the key through the window. He was supposed to come back every few hours to relieve us, but when he got busy he often forgot. Mary couldn't stand it. When it was time for her break, she was willing to take a chance on anyone, anyone at all to let us out. It didn't matter that her window was crawling with marks. Mary just wanted out. I was hoping that our new truce might make her more reasonable, but we fought over the key the first day—you might have thought I was hitting her, she was yelling so loud—and we fought again the next. After that, I kept my mouth shut. I did not want to fight. Now that we were starting to get along, I didn't see the point. I let her have the key whenever she looked restless. She never asked why, never said thank you. Sometimes she was gone only a few minutes, but other times she was gone all afternoon. She never told me where she went, and I never asked. I was just glad she came back. We never said anything about it at all.

We worked hard. When kids come to have fun, they act like animals. Slap their hands away, tell them to slow down, shut up, line up or die, but they never listen. They want the fair, they want their ride. As long as they get their tickets, they don't care about the rest of it. They came that summer in crumbling church buses and they ran to our windows with hands full of money, shouting and laughing and banging on the walls. Sometimes there were so many of them pressing forward that the wheels of our booth came unlocked. If they made a game of rolling us back and forth across the parking lot, we didn't mind—it was a relief from the boredom—but there was a day somewhere in the heat of mid-July when a gang of kids from Springer showed up. They didn't come to our windows, they went around to the side. I knew what they wanted. So did Mary. When we felt ourselves moving, we held onto each other for balance and I whispered, make a joke of it, tell them it's funny, tell them we're having a ball. It was a good idea, but Mary started laughing too hard, taking it too seriously, and when we bumped over the cattle guard past the front gate she pulled away from me, stood up, grabbed the bars in both hands, and screamed. It was a terrible scream, more animal than human. I clapped my hands over my ears to stop it. Screaming can make you feel all hope in the world is gone. When we stopped moving, two of Fun's bouncers were running towards us, scattering gigglers into the sagebrush, but I was so angry I could barely breathe. Our booth was in the middle of the road, only twenty yards from where we'd started. Mary was still holding the bars. "Thanks a lot," I whispered. "What'd you think, they were going to push us out to the highway? We're not even close. Now they're going to call us yellow for the rest of our lives." But Mary looked as if a vial of blood had broken behind her eyes. "Liar," she hissed. "You wanted me to scream. You were waiting for it. You made me scream so you wouldn't have to."

I don't know. Maybe she was right. The truth is, when you work a fair and have to listen to people screaming for

fun on the rides all around you day in and day out, you do kind of get the itch to hear a real scream for once. Just once, just so you can be sure you still know the difference. There's nothing uncaring about it. It's just part of being bored. It's just this idea you get when you are seventeen and working in one room all summer long that a real scream will make the hours move a little faster. Or maybe it was only that I was so used to things being crazy with Mick that I was beginning to wonder if in some way they weren't still crazy without him. Maybe I was trying to find out. I don't know. And now that Mick's gone and Mary's gone, too, what's to happen if the situation ever gets to the point of a scream again? Do I have to be the one?

In August when we heard Mick had been sent up to Marion, Ohio, I spotted his girlfriend in the midway, the one he had thought would bring him luck. Willa Moon. She was with Lee Fiddle and she was laughing like she'd been drinking all day, like she'd never seen such a good time. I meant to tell Mary when she got back from her break, but I forgot because Fun Harrison stopped by to say that he was switching Mother and me over to the night shift. To my surprise, he wanted to switch Mary over, too. "Don't you think she's a little young?" I said. "Night work's a different world. She's never done it before." But I didn't push it. We needed the money, and besides, I was having reservations about leaving Mary alone to work the day shift. She was growing more unpredictable. Not answering questions or comments, sometimes not talking for hours, just staring out the window, not even bothering to be polite. The idea of her being alone in the trailer at night bothered me. Besides, I told her, working the night shift was something you had to share to appreciate. No more church groups, no Cub Scouts and Brownies, no squally babies looking for mothers. At night, the kiddie rides were closed, the neon hydraulics of the Blaster lit up, the beer tent was packed, and the sign at the front gate saying Howdy Kids! was turned around so that it read No Unaccompanied Minors Allowed. For protection, our booth was rolled into the heart of the midway and Fun's bouncers carried electric cattle prods in their belts. Mary wouldn't be allowed out on breaks alone, but I told her she wouldn't mind because at night in the booth anything could happen. A man with no ears might appear at your window, a kid with no hands who poked his elbows through the bars, a dwarf or a clubfoot, a woman with gold teeth. They shuffled by as if on parade, but because I kept the light inside the booth unscrewed, all they could see of us were our hands reaching through the bars for their money. We didn't have to wear our work beanies, we didn't have to smile, we didn't have to worry about people recognizing us as Mick Angel's sisters. With the calliope drowning us out, we could say or do anything we wanted. We were invisible. All we had to do was take their money. "Relax, Mar," I said as I braided all that wild red hair of hers in two nice straight lines down her back. "Once you get used to them coming at you like that, once you know how to deal with it, it's like sitting home with the lights off, watching 'Animal Kingdom' on TV."

But about twenty minutes into the first night, I knew I had made a mistake. Mary was too curious for what she didn't understand, too high-strung to sit still and watch. She wanted more. She always had. She wanted to talk with the Mexican beet pickers, she wanted to touch the freaks. When a drunk with something hanging off the end of his nose stag-

gered up to my window and asked if anybody was home, she started to giggle, started to rise off the bench. I pushed her back down to her seat but she shoved me away. "Hey, mister," she called. "Over here. Come around to my window. I'll talk to you."

I ignored her after that. I let her do and say anything she wanted, at least until she reached up to screw in the overhead light in the booth. "What do you think you're doing?" I cried, unscrewing the bulb. "They can see us."

"So?" She screwed the light back in. And when the next group of marks stepped into the lights of the midway, three boys in shined-up cowboy boots, new cowboy hats, and flowered shirts, Mary began to taunt them. "Come on," she called, giggling and half crouched at her window, "You afraid of us? Come on, you cowpoke fruits. Come closer." They did—and trailing behind them, two from Stygo I recognized, Lizzy and Jake Loper, people I'd gone to school with—but the whole group being drunk as monkeys, none of them seemed to recognize us, or care. Lizzy Loper was so gone she couldn't even remember what tickets were for. Part of me wanted to slap Mary away from the window, turn off the light and yell at her until she cried; but the other part of me wanted to win. I felt I had a right to it for once. "That's nothing," I said and when I saw Sy Peske hurrying by on his way to the beer tent, I leaned against the bars and asked if he wanted to come over and touch my face. It was a safe bet— Peske turns deaf as a post when he needs a drink—but Mary was impressed. To hide it, she turned back to her own window. "Nice try, Essie," she said, leaning forward towards an idiot with no eyebrows who was trying to count his fingers. "But watch this."

That was how the game started. If I taught a group of wet-backs to say "shit you" instead of "thank you," Mary made the blind kid who showed up with Pearl Stiles grope for her change. If I told old Billy Quail, the Yiwa, that we wanted to marry him, Mary told him we wanted to fuck. It was the kind of game that has its own rhythm and secrets, and the more we did it the harder it was to stop. Old marks, ugly marks, drunk marks, marks who knew us and marks who didn't, amputees, Jehovah's Witnesses, even a priest. After a while it was anyone who came for a ticket, anyone. We didn't turn off the light and we never said we were sorry. If they started howling, we called Fun's bouncers to cart them away. Mary was more reckless than me—when she got excited she couldn't stop—but she was loyal to me now, which meant more often than not that when she lost control, she would burst out with what I had been thinking as if we shared the same mind. We didn't need anyone else. It was a wonderful discovery. We stopped fighting each other altogether.

But as the month wore on, I felt something growing between us in the booth. As if we were gathering all the heat and noise of the summer inside us, as if we could not let it go. Towards the end of August, I started easing up a little, letting Mary take the lead. I was having nightmares. Not like Mary's—about Funtown or Mick coming back or the light in winter out beyond the last trailer—but all those people bunching up to our windows at night, trying to talk over the shriek of the calliope. Sometimes I dreamt that Mary was gone and I'd fallen asleep in the booth, that the faces outside were pressing against the windows, slipping through the bars to pry open my mouth. On nights like that I woke up still

tasting the dust of their fingers, the smell of their breath in the sheet.

I don't know why Mother didn't stop us. She must have known, if not from hearing us then at least from our laughter, the shrieking, hyena laughter coming from the booth. But she was always polishing her bottles or tidying her shelves, iron-faced as a sleepwalker. I knew what she was thinking. Each night a smaller crowd, a little quieter, a little calmer, the neon arms of the Blaster rising and falling in the dark, its rockets indifferent and bright. The midway would fill up and empty out and fill up, but come October the midway would be empty, Fun's calliope shut down, the Blaster dark and silent, the booths cleaned and boarded up, the people gone. She was counting on it. As the end of the season drew near and business started dwindling back down to locals from Stygo, she began to cheer up a little, stopping by our booth when she knew we weren't playing the game. "How's tricks?" she'd say, dusting off the bars. "Having a good time, girls?" I don't know what got into Mary and me. We loved her, of course, and appreciated the fact that she was trying her best to patch together our family; but the minute she left and three Vietnam vets showed up in wheelchairs at our windows for tickets, we told them we were prisoners, that we wanted them to save us, that they had to get us out.

The last week of the season, the calliope broke. Since we didn't expect much more business before winter, it didn't really matter. But we had been talking over the music all season, its rhythm and whine a part of our blood, and to have it stop, to suddenly have nothing—it was like losing a part of your mind. An empty fair at night is an unlikable place when there's no music to cover the sounds of machinery. There's nothing to cut time into parts you can handle, nothing to tell you time is passing at all. The roustabouts could wander up and down the midway, the barkers could hide behind their counters to play cards and drink, but Mary and I had nothing at all. We unscrewed the overhead light so we could see farther out into the dark, but it didn't help. Nobody came. We discussed all the ways we'd played the game so far, all the ways still left to play it, but after a night or two, we were fighting again, worse than ever. I told her I was sorry I'd ever agreed to let her work nights with me and she said she was sorry I'd ever been born. The third night Fun threatened to fire us if we didn't end up killing each other first.

But after he stormed off, a group of half-wits from Mason City wandered in from the parking lot down at the far end of the midway. Mary and I both stood up. Some were old and some not so old, and they entered the midway bumping up against each other, holding on, shying away from the lights, staring like fish.

I thought about letting Mary take them. I don't like half-wits. One or two are all right, but when they come in groups they tend to crowd both windows at once, knocking into each other like wound-up toys, those soft, damp hands of theirs reaching out for the tickets. Hands that are too long or too short, too white or too pink, too fat or too thin, too nervous or too still to touch. You never know what half-wits are thinking, what they're capable of. But Mary was so sure I'd let her have them that I couldn't resist.

"Haven't you forgotten something?" pushing her behind me. "It's my turn."

She looked ready to rip out the bars. "Goddamn you," she

snarled, staring out at the group in the midway. "This better be good."

"Here's what. We ask two bucks for every ticket." She jerked around to me. "Two-fifty," I added.

"Oh God." She slumped back on the bench, staring darkly out the window at the half-wits.

"What."

She turned to me, all that heat burning in her eyes. "You want to use our one possibly last chance at a fun night by asking for something as boring as a fucking extra buck-fifty?"

"Oh," I said, sitting behind her. "I get it. You're chicken. Okay. I'll do it alone."

"Chicken?" She pointed to the window. "You think I'm chicken to ask them for money? They don't even know what money is. They don't even care."

She was right—bunched together at the center of the midway, the half-wits seemed to have no idea what they were supposed to do next—but as we watched them, I could feel the sting of being wrong building inside me, charging around looking for a way out. When I found it, my hands felt as if I'd dipped them in ice. "Let's play the game then," I said. I reached for the key hanging on the nail below my counter. "Too bad you're too young to take breaks at night, Mar. I'm going to follow them."

Mary spun as if she'd been slapped. "Follow them? You mean—follow them?" She began to giggle. "Oh God!" She grabbed the key from me and leaned to her window. "Hey, Billy," she shouted. "Billy Fiddle. You know where Fun went? We want a break."

"Not you." I snatched back the key. "You're only fourteen. You're not allowed to go on breaks alone."

"But you're with me," she said. When I did not answer she grabbed my arm. "What are you talking about? We're in this together. You can't leave me here."

"Why not?" I said, realizing as I turned to her that the astonishment I saw in her face was what I'd tried for all summer, what I'd always hated Mick for taking first from Mary. "Remember all the breaks you took this summer?" I said. "You left me in here lots of times by myself. Why can't I leave you now?"

"But this is the *game!*" she burst out. But then she stopped and her eyes turned dark and for a moment there was a violence between us that ticked. I thought she was going to hit me and there was a part of me eager to have it. But instead she brought her fist down on my ticket dispenser and it fell, smacking against my knee cap.

I yelled in pain. "What'd you do that for?"

"You're not going to do anything," she hissed. "You're just going to pretend you did. You always do it that way. You're chicken."

"Who says so?"

Mary stopped short, narrowing her eyes.

"I said who says so."

"Mick," she whispered. "Mick said you were a chicken. He said you were the biggest chicken in this whole county."

There was a silence in the booth. I turned back to the window. "Okay," I said. "You asked for it."

They weren't that frightening when you studied them from a certain point of view. They were dressed like a team, light blue wind breakers and gray sweatpants and tan jogging shoes and on every one the same haircut—fierce and short, as if someone had placed a bowl over their heads and chopped around it. They were trying to stay together, trying to keep track and not get lost. One of them was crying. He was about my age and he was trying to shake an old woman off his arm. He was sobbing, as if the world was over, but when he looked in my direction, his eyes turned as blank as the bottom of a pan. It gave me an uneasy feeling. No, I wouldn't talk to him. I looked over at the Three-A-Shot. Mother was watching them, too, cradling her tip jar in one hand while the other flew around like a moth trapped inside, wiping the glass with a rag. She hated nights like this. I looked down the midway. Sarah and Rosa Zambini at the Drop-A-Dime were watching and so were their marks, Billy Quail and Frank Stiles and behind them in the shadows, Billy's daughter, Kwami, sucking on a molasses stick. Everyone was watching except Brice Jopa and Sy Peske who were bent over up to their elbows in calliope pipes, trying to fix the music. Down at the end, I saw Fun Harrison hurry across the midway carrying a cattle prod.

I could feel Mary over my shoulder. When I turned, her eyes were two points of light, her mouth open, everything focused and ready and still. She didn't look like Mary anymore. She had a look in her eyes I knew nothing about.

"We take them on a ride," she whispered. "The Viper. Or the Black-Out, show them the mirrors—"

"*I* decide what we do," I said. I clenched my jaw. "We sell them tickets first. For double the price. Then we get out and follow them. But we do it my way. It's my idea."

"Shit!" She grabbed the bars. "They've got that snitch, Whatly, with them. And he's already got tickets for them."

At that distance I might not have recognized Oren Whatly

except that he was wearing the same green baseball cap with the sheriff's badge pinned to it that he'd worn the night he'd arrived on our doorstep with the FBI. He was standing in front of the group with a cigarette dangling from the corner of his mouth and handing out tickets. When he turned, I saw he'd pinned one of Mama Jewell Peske's We Care buttons on the back of his cap.

"Shit," said Mary.

"Take it easy. So they got a cop with them. So?" I glanced at her from the side. "I guess that's it, though. I mean—"

"Jesus," she whispered. "Look at them."

They were crowding him, slobbering, holding their hands out for their ticket. Some put it under their hats or crumpled it into their hands. One man folded his ticket into his mouth like a stick of gum. His eyes were hammered into his head like nails sunk deep into wood. Oren Whatly tapped him on the shoulder. "Nick?" The man turned, openmouthed, staring at Oren as if he was God. They all did. Oren picked the ticket off the man's tongue and handed it to him again. "Thank you, sir" the man said.

"Holy shit. That's Harley Barrows' dad," whispered Mary. "Mick helped him repaint the boarding house in Stygo a couple years ago. Mick never got paid. Remember?"

"No."

"I do. Jeez. Poor Mr. Barrows." Mary was quiet.

I looked out the window. "They shouldn't bring people like that to Funtown, though. Anything could happen." When Mary said nothing I looked over at her. "Mary?"

"What," she breathed. But I did not know what I wanted except for her to turn and look at me, which she did not, so I did not answer.

"Yo. Riders," called Oren. I turned back to the window as he clapped twice. "Heads up. Stay together." He turned and started walking and they followed in panic, knocking against each other and grabbing on, trying to keep together and keep him in sight, their mouths open like baby birds.

"Hi, girls." Fun was at the other window, his fat pink face filling it, the corners of his mouth stretched wide to show the gaps between his teeth as he squinted into the dark of our booth. "Fiddle says you were looking for me."

"We want to go on break," said Mary, leaping to the window. "Essie's going too. Here." She pushed the key under the bars. When he did not take it, she leaned forward, screwing up her eyes, ready for a fight. "What."

"Nothing," he said, the joke in his voice. "Just want to know why you want out so bad all of a sudden. I'm not supposed to let wild animals out of their cages at night."

I could feel Mary tighten. She slid sideways and shoved me forward to the window.

"Well?" said Fun.

"We want to go on break," I said. "Like she said."

Fun poked his black tongue out the corner of his mouth and squinted down the midway. He liked me, he always said he could trust me like a daughter, and I could feel Mary beside me now, daring me to use it and already turning against me because she thought I would not, her eyes in the dark like Mick's, watching me, blaming me for being weak, for not wanting enough, for holding her back. Things had gone too far. But when I glanced out the other window, I saw that the midway was empty again, Billy Fiddle and the other bouncers leaning back, relaxed now, picking at their hands.

"Come on, Fun." I put my hand up to the bars. "We're

not going to do anything. Honor's cross. We have to use the bathroom."

He turned and looked at Mary, who stared back out through the bars at him. "Oh lord." He took the key and started around to the side, but then he came back. "You listen to me now, Essie Angel. I'm not putting up with trouble. Not the way I used to with your brother. Understood?"

I nodded.

Fun sighed, spat out a plug of tobacco and went around to the door.

"See?" I whispered.

But Mary wasn't listening. She had her back to me, staring at the door, waiting for it to spring open.

■

It was a relief to be out in the midway. Things came into focus again. I felt light-headed and clear. Nothing was going to happen. Mary just wanted out. She let out a laugh and waved to Mother who had turned away, and as soon as we were past the Three-A-Shot, she grabbed my wrist and we began to run.

Oren Whatly led them straight to the Wheel of Light, the brightest ride in Funtown, second in height only to the Blaster. I pulled Mary around to the dark side by the exit ramp. The Zambini girls were already there and so were Fun's roustabouts, including Ralph and Pokey, Fun's nephews. A woman stepped out of the shadows on the far side of the Wheel—Willa Moon back for more fun. I watched her stroll past the half-wits and on down the midway arm in arm with Zene Gercer, who was falling all over himself trying to make conversation. Willa Moon was laughing, her head thrown back. It came as a relief to me that

Mary didn't notice. She was too busy watching the half-wits on the platform as they waited for the Wheel to stop and let them on. I looked around. Everybody was watching. It reminded me of the night the summer before when Mick had gotten into a fight with Billy Fiddle. It was a sudden fight, loud and bloody, and when I told Mick afterwards I hated him for it, in truth what I hated was not that he had almost killed Billy, but that he had let people watch him lose control, people who did not care in the least what Mick Angel believed in and what he wanted and what he could never have. It was an old memory but it did not feel old. It felt fresh and true. But then I was back again and Mary and the others were beside me and this was frumpy Oren Whatly we were watching. A gumbo, a snitch, a babysitter of nuts, a cop who couldn't even afford a uniform. He was across the loading platform from us, squinting up through the smoke of his cigarette at the Wheel, waiting for it to stop. His half-wits stood behind him, their eyes glued to the back of his hat. I don't think they saw us. I don't think they even knew where they were. All they could do was stare at Oren Whatly. When John Wackett gave him the sign, he put out his cigarette and stepped through the gate. I felt hard and cold. Who did he think he was, putting half-wits on the Wheel? It was not just dangerous, it was stupid. They bumped through the gate like sheep entering the chute, miserable and confused, staring at Oren, unable to bear the rest of it. No, I thought, he deserved it if someone panicked and fell. Even John Wackett thought so. He was supposed to collect tickets and warn them about safety, but he stood off to one side, hanging off his crutch, his face tight with disgust. Oren separated a man and a woman from the rest of the group and helped them into a car. The woman cried out and began to pat her face as if she did not know what it was. Oren touched her shoulder, said something and then stepped back, smiling. John Wackett hobbled forward, slammed their safety bar down without a word and stormed back to the operator's switch box. As the Wheel groaned into gear, the half-wits in the car lurched in their seats and cried out, trying to stand up to see where Oren had gone. Rosa Zambini gasped, but her sister, who was my age, did not. I turned and met her eyes in the dark. Sarah had not been a friend of mine before.

"What do you bet one of them tries to climb out of the car when it gets up to the top?" I said out of the corner of my mouth. "Blood everywhere." Sarah's eyes widened and we both giggled. Pokey Harrison nudged me in the back.

"If they do, you better get Mick Jr. out of the way first. She's liable to get flattened."

I turned. Mary had moved forward to the edge of the platform, her fingers laced in the red chainlink. She was staring up at Oren Whatly, close enough to reach out and touch his boot. He was taking care of them, easing them into their cars like they were made of china, sending them off with a tip of his hat. Somewhere up above near the top of the wheel, one of them had started to cry. I stepped forward and hit Mary in the back. "Hey. You're too close. Back up." Mary's spine was rigid, her red hair wild and tangled in the back as if she'd slept on it. When she didn't turn, I hit her again.

Mary turned slowly. She looked at Sarah and Rosa, Pokey and Ralph and then she looked at me. "No," she said. "You just think what everybody else thinks. Leave me alone."

I looked up at Oren Whatly. He had everyone on the Wheel now, and he was climbing in the last car with Mr. Barrows. I watched them and the way Mary was staring at them. No, I liked the situation. It was interesting. When the great neon arms of the Wheel began to move, I stepped up behind Mary. "This is it," I shouted, grabbing her arm. "Watch, Mary. This is where it happens."

But nobody fell. Off they floated into the dark, two by two and sometimes three, their faces set like waxed paper. Some came back around looking like they'd passed an angel on the way and some like they were being tortured. The thing was, you couldn't hear them. Any of them. There was no sound, just the growl and screech of the Wheel, the great arms of metal rubbing against metal. All of them had their mouths open, they were all trying to do something, but you couldn't tell if it was screaming or laughing or crying for help. They could have been feeling anything. It was like looking through a soundproof window at people living through and falling out of their entire lives in the space of one three-minute ride. It made me so dizzy that when Mary jerked away from me, I almost fell. Under the neon her hair was purple-red, her face pale as the moon. She opened her mouth. "You want them to fall," she shouted. "You want it."

"What did you want?" I called but I couldn't hear myself for all the noise of the machinery and I couldn't stand the way she was looking at me. I pushed through the open-mouthed crowd behind me and ran back to our booth.

We did not talk about it. We sat in the booth, staring out opposite windows, watching the workers drift back to their jobs to close up for the night. When I saw Oren Whatly heading back out towards the parking lot with his group, I didn't tell Mary but she must have spotted them herself. "What," I said. "They didn't get hurt. They didn't lose a drop of blood. They had fun." But she covered her face and cried and would not answer me at all, and though she stopped when Fun came to let us out at the end of our shift, everything was changed. I knew it. I could feel it. The next night she would not even trade glances with me when a man with no nose asked us the time. She was silent, she did her job, and if I tried so much as a passing remark, she stared at me as if she didn't know who I was. "How do you expect to put up with this place?" I said. "Fuck you, Mary. You're not so different from the rest of us. You just think you are." But Mary wouldn't even fight. "Never mind," I said. "I'm not sorry. You're as crazy as Mick was. You're crazy, that's what I think." And at the end of the week, when Fun's truckers came in to tear down the rides for winter and Mary talked one of them into taking her with him, I knew I'd been right. Mary was crazy. She had always believed in what didn't exist. She could never grow up. We waited for a letter but it never came. Mother cried for her and cursed Mick for having poisoned her against us.

I cried too, eventually. But it was not about Mary. It was about Mother and me and what we had left.

EIGHT

SOMETHING TO GO BY

SOMETHING
TO GO BY

The storm began in the morning, but it wasn't until late in the afternoon, with winds blasting at the door and drifts creeping up the window on the north side of the cabin, that Billy Fiddle got the call from Sheriff Whatly in Stygo saying they needed him on the plow. "We just heard the truckers are doubling back to Mason City," said Oren. "Route 34's about gone. So I guess if you feel like it, Billy, we could use your help. I'll make sure the county reimburses you for your time."

"Whatever. Just don't forget to buy me a drink when I get there."

"Hold on." Oren put his hand over the receiver, arguing with someone in the background. A moment later, Frank Stiles came on. "I wouldn't mind coming out there and doing it myself, Bill," said Frank, "only I got problems of my own here. My dog wandered off. Broke her rope. Maybe it was worn through. I don't know." He paused. "Betsy's awful damn old. If I don't go looking for her, she might not find her way home." The storm crackled through the connection, bringing the sound of a voice talking on another line far away. "If you're not up to this, Billy, we can send Sy out to your place. We asked him the other day and he says he can drive a plow—"

"Peske wouldn't know the starter button from the brake," said Billy. "He never drove a blade in his life."

There was a pause. "We're not saying you have to do it. Forget the plow if you want. You're not on contract. Just come on into Stygo anyway before you get yourself snowed in out there. Oren's got a poker game going—you can take my place—"

"Are you worried about me, Frank? Is that why you're calling?"

"No, Bill, we—"

Billy threw the phone down on the bed and went to the kitchen for a cigarette. Frank was tiptoeing around again, he could feel it. All that careful politeness, all that cheerful, we understand shit that sometimes made Billy so crazy he wanted to drive into town with Lee's old baseball bat and bust out everybody's windows. What did they think he was anyway, jello and chalk? Two months now without his twin brother, Lee, two months and he'd managed fine—no weepy fits when he stopped in town for supplies, no pathetic scenes or threats or late night calls for help—but as far as Frank was concerned, it was only a matter of time. He went back to the phone and picked up the receiver. "You guys want me to clear the roads or not?"

A startled silence at the other end. "Yeah, Bill. I guess."

Billy dressed meticulously. Though he'd worked for days to get the plow ready, ignoring his other chores, he had not yet figured out how to fix the heater. The cold would seep through the glass cage like milk through bread. Layer on layer, nylon over cotton, wool over nylon, wool over wool. The overhead bulb flickered on and off. By the time he'd gone through both his and Lee's bureaus to find two gloves that matched, he was sweating behind his knees and under his arms. He put on a pair of socks, wrapped his feet in thermal Plasti-Wrap, put on another pair of socks, and finally, tugged on his boots.

He had to hunt through the bed clothes for the cap to the bottle of Red Spot. He screwed it on and put the bottle in the pocket of his Air Force parka. In the kitchen, he searched the mess on the counters for the key to the plow and a roll of antacid tablets. He filled the thermos with coffee, stoked the stove with piñon, opened the tap to a drip, and stuffed an old sweater of Lee's under the back door. The thermometer outside the kitchen window read ten below. God knows how cold it was out on the highway. He tied the hood of his parka in a knot under his chin, zipped on his gloves, picked up the pry bar on the kitchen table, and after a last look around to make sure he had not forgotten anything, he turned off the light, opened the front door and stepped out.

The storm was wild, slapping him against the side of the house as if it didn't want him to leave. He padlocked the door and started across the yard towards the barn, one arm up to see and the other following the guide rope. In places he sank past his knees. Frank and Oren had probably wasted hours trying to figure out some way of not asking Billy at all. "Christ on a crutch," said Billy aloud. "You might think I had a disease. Lee was the one with the disease. He's the one who croaked."

Billy didn't mind saying it out loud. He liked the way it changed things, the way it put the truth in perspective. Saying it out loud was like playing Russian Roulette and finding after you pull the trigger that your head is still in one piece. Besides, what kind of respect could you keep for yourself if you couldn't call a spade a spade? The first time he'd tried it, he'd been alone in the washroom at the hospital in Mason City. He was leaning over to wash his face and as a sort of experiment he'd said to the mirror, "Lee's a goner." Afterwards, he'd gone back out to the lounge area where Frank and his sister Jewell and Oren were waiting and said it to them. The shock on their faces, the denial and shame and most of all, the pop of dislike for Billy that jumped out before they could stop themselves, all of it told Billy he was right. Not only were people afraid of the truth, they couldn't handle it. In fact, most people despised Billy from that moment on. Frank especially, though he hid his dislike by telling everyone what Billy needed was pity. But it was Frank who needed pity. Cracking the truth was a sort of test, like holding your hand over an open flame or eating habañeros chilis raw or staring the guy next to you into a fight. Whenever Billy said it out loud, he felt as sanctified against hurt as if he'd encased himself in steel.

He kicked through the last drift to the barn. Using the pry bar to crack the ice on the doors, he pulled them apart enough to squeeze inside. Bracing himself against them, he pushed them open one at a time, ramming back the snow. The wind was against him and it was hard work. If he had waited much longer, he might not have been able to get the doors open at all. He circled the plow, tapping tread with the pry bar. He could hear his breathing behind him in the barn like someone else.

The plow had been Lee's idea—he'd spent every dime he'd had to meet the first payment—but it was Billy who had figured out the fuel-line problem and got her going on her own power. Lee wasn't the mechanical type; he just wanted to own a plow. Last October, when everybody else was bringing Lee candy and get-well cards in the hospital, it was Billy who brought Lee what he wanted to see, the receipts of plow payments kept up to date. Billy had rewired the headlights, cleaned the carburetor, serviced the spool valves, and replaced the glow plugs with his own money. And when Doc Seymour said Lee wouldn't be getting out that winter, let alone the next, it was Billy who had taken the initiative to learn how to drive and manipulate the blade. Stygo's town council didn't offer to send him to driving school like they had Lee. They didn't even mention it. Billy just did it, the same way Lee would have done it for him if their positions had been reversed. Every day before he went to Funtown to work he went out to practice on the plow, and he'd gotten good at it, too, good enough to make a mound out on the flats east of town that was bigger than any bump on the landscape for miles around. When he was done, he'd planted a sign on top of it saying Fiddle's Tit, and took a Polaroid of it to show to Lee. Lee was in bad shape by then and everybody who knew it looked at Billy when he came to the hospital with the picture as if he was to blame for it. But Lee understood. Lee laughed so hard he nearly blew out his intravenous tubes. He told Oren and Frank to make the town council vote in Fiddle's Tit as the county's first official landmark. Why not? said Frank. But after the funeral, nobody wanted to remember what Lee wanted. Turning up daisies had scared them away. That kind of thing didn't scare Billy. "Not me, Bucko." Next Fourth of July he was going to go out there and make the Tit official himself. Shoot fireworks off it, maybe re-do the sign, bigger this time, in red, so you could see the name from the highway.

Billy opened the cab, stepped on the running board and swung himself inside. It was the biggest machine on the road, a landmark in itself, dwarfing cars and trucks the way Godzilla dwarfed towns and villages. Everything was over-sized: the steering wheel, the windows, the pedals and the shift balls, the huge hydraulic arms rising and falling, react-ing in kind to the slightest touch. Two thousand pounds pressure per square inch in the hydraulic fluid line, that was what Jake Loper had told him, that's what Billy drove with the shove and punch of a shift. Touch the wrong lever and you could take out a car, swipe down a telephone pole, shave the porch off a house. Billy pushed the starter button and the engine roared.

Held within the barn, the sound of the engine was deaf-ening. Outside the doors the blizzard glowed like the moon. He adjusted the choke and put her in gear, but when he backed off the clutch she bucked towards the doorway and quit, nearly throwing him off the seat. He cursed, pulled out the choke, and started the engine again, waiting this time for it to warm up. A cloud of diesel rose, circled around the barn until it found the door, and fled.

He felt ready to suffocate under all his layers. He pushed back the hood of his parka and glanced in the rearview. His face looked bloated, eyes bulging like two fish straining to get out of a net of red threads. He pulled off his gloves, took out the bottle of Red Spot and held it to the light. If Frank and Oren hadn't made him wait all morning, Billy wouldn't have had to drink so much. Waiting made him nervous. It had always made him nervous, but now that Lee wasn't around, waiting had become a pain in the ass. Billy drank, not because he needed it to feel good, the way Lee had needed it, but because liquor measured out waiting in amounts you could deal with. One drink's worth, two drinks' worth, three, and so on—until the waiting was over, until you could put away the bottle and get on with it again.

While he waited, he turned on the headlights. No cabin, no woodpile, no highway, not even the mile marker post. Everything was gone. He closed his eyes and took a pull, then put the bottle away and worked his gloves on. "Come on, sister." When he tapped on the gas, the engine responded. He reached under the seat for his hunting cap and pulled it on, patting the wool flaps down over his ears. "Okay all you gophers out there. Duck your heads." He dropped the blade, eased the plow into first, and keeping one foot on the brake to prevent the engine getting away, he chugged out into the yard.

The storm howled into the headlights. He might as well have been blind. It wasn't until he felt the blade scraping hardscrabble that he realized he'd come to the edge of the highway. He paused to shake the tension out of his shoulders and arms and pulled down his cap. He took a deep breath to loosen his chest, breathed out hard, and then turned the front wheels slowly east towards Stygo.

This was his first real weather job and he had to concentrate. He might lose his sense of direction. He might veer off course, hit a mileage marker, wind up spending the night in some irrigation ditch. It occurred to him that if he kept an eye on the scraped pavement behind the blade instead of looking for the road up ahead, the white guideline on the shoulder of highway would give him something to go by. He tried this and made better time.

He began to breathe easier. Once or twice he tried "Oh Suzanna," doctoring verses as he went along. His refrain was lost in the engine, in the high, brutal whine of wind squeezing through the crack in the windshield. It was blizzarding from the ground up. To stay alert he kept his eyes moving. The rearview, the crack in the windshield, the headlights, the trace of white guideline just behind the blade. There was nothing up ahead. No treadmarks, no taillights, no landmarks. On a night like this, Frank's old dog was lost for sure. Billy felt as if he was sitting in a narrow box with sides made not of windows but of pale gray wood. He craned forward, squinting hard. He might miss the Stygo turn-off sign. He might end up without knowing it driving all the way to Miami. Rum punch at the beach. Bikinis. The Dolphins. Have Frank and all the other sap-guts in Stygo get a load of him on TV next Sunday.

It was only ten miles to town, straight as a beam of light, but the going was slow. He was beginning to feel the cold crawl up his arms and legs beneath the layers of clothing, fuddling his senses. He kept forgetting himself, kept losing himself in the blizzard as it came into his headlights and then swerving in panic, thinking he'd seen a deer running towards him, the taillights of a car, a jack-knifed semi, a sudden drop-off in the road up ahead. When he leaned forward to wipe the inside of the windshield with a rag, a pink-cheeked, open-mouthed baby rolled out of the white swirl into the blade.

He slid to a stop. He put the plow in neutral, pulled off his gloves, poured some coffee from the thermos and drank it down, burning his tongue and throat.

He'd started picturing Lee again. Not the Lee in bed,

which was how Billy usually thought of him—shrunken and chicken-skinned, nothing but a bump under sheets, with tubes running everywhere, with eyes like butterbeans, like someone Billy'd never seen before, someone twice as old as Billy—but Lee his twin brother, smiling and picking his teeth with a match. Lee after dinner tilting back in his chair to drink and then laughing so hard at Billy's joke he tipped over, holding himself and slapping the porch, banging the bottle and crying stop, stop, I can't hardly breathe. And the girl, Stephy, just standing there in the kitchen doorway looking down over that swollen belly and that push-up bra of hers that fooled you and that voice like acid, "You coming to bed or what." But Lee couldn't stop, not once Billy got him going. "Aw, honeybuck," he said, still laughing and trying to get up and back in his chair. "You just don't understand my brother. You just don't." And as far as Billy knew, that was as close as Lee ever came to telling Stephy she was wrong to have picked him, that she should have stayed with that little dried-up pissant, Donald What's-his-name who was waiting for her back in Albuquerque, where at least her dried-up little heart wouldn't have had to feel so out of place.

But then the baby came and it was Lee telling Billy to shut up and meaning it, holding the baby bottle in one hand and diapers in the other and trying to be everything for Lee, Jr., that he knew he was not. Jesus. He was so busy worrying over the little yellow shits and two A.M. feedings he couldn't even laugh when he drank. Stephy watched, calculating everything like an adding machine, and when he started getting headaches and falling down for no reason, when Doc Seymour said it was not just the drinking but something else, something worse, she narrowed her eyes, rang the Total button and was gone the next day with the baby. Lee couldn't believe it. He couldn't believe it for four days and on the fifth, he got drunk. As drunk as Billy had seen him, crawling down the stairs, following the walls, howling and tearing up the house in search of the shotgun to shoot himself with. But Billy knew what Lee needed. He threw the gun out in Sam Waters' corn field, left a bottle of Red Spot on the table, and drove all the way to Denver to buy Lee $200 worth of pale green lizardskin boots. By the time he got back, Lee was in the hospital and the nurses who didn't know Lee had an identical twin stared at Billy like he was Death itself riding into the X-ray room. All Lee did was ask where Billy had been for two days and what the hell did he expect him to do with a pair of goddamn lizard boots? But Billy just grinned. Lee was tangled up in pity. He was out of his head. "I don't know," said Billy. "Maybe you'll get laid or something. What do you think, Nurse?" And Lee, looking down at himself so sorryful in that paper dress they'd put him in and those gleamy green boots on his feet, had looked over at Billy and started laughing. That's why Billy had gotten them, because Lee wasn't ready to stop laughing yet, wasn't ready for the truth they were all trying to bury him with, because what Lee needed was to go home and sit out on the porch with his brother like it was any other night, like all the best nights of their lives, Lee banging those new shiny green boots on the porch and bucking back in his chair to howl at the punch line. Billy wanted to lift the blade and turn off the engine, stop the noise for just five minutes. But he yanked down the bill of his cap and went on, afraid if he shut her down she might not re-start. The storm sounded like it wanted to come inside. It sounded like some kind of animal.

A lot of the nurses on the fifth floor had been damn good-looking. If Lee had gotten well he could have had his pick. Billy remembered one in particular, a candy striper who came one day to get the lizardskin boots off Lee for an X-ray of his feet and couldn't and was about to panic over it until Billy closed the door to the hallway and showed her how, the three of them giggling as she bent over, her hair coming loose and Lee's one boot planted on her rumble seat while she held the other between her legs and pulled. She was something to look at—all strawberries and cream with hair the curliest, reddish-purple color he'd ever seen—hair that in all that hospital whiteness had been a sort of landmark for him during those last awful days. She had been nicer than Stephy in a hundred ways. He was sorry he couldn't remember her last name. He drove on, wondering if she remembered him, wondering if she remembered Billy Fiddle as a good time or just the twin brother of some guy who'd kicked, and then he was back, the exit sign to Stygo springing up in his headlights with the suddenness of an oncoming truck. He cried out and slammed on the brake, veering into the center of the road.

Billy looked back at the sign or what he could make of it through the blizzard. It was lucky he had spotted it at all. He took off his gloves and had a drink. When he screwed on the cap, his hands were shaking. He had difficulty getting his gloves back on.

He curved off the highway onto the road into Stygo. He stayed on the right guideline, keeping a sharp eye out for the Conoco sign, but the first building he came to was the Stygo Grand, looming up on his left. He'd passed the gas station without even knowing it. The rest of the town appeared building by building, all of it dark and howling with drifts leaning against doorways. Not one car out tonight, not one person. Billy tightened his jaw. Bums. They would all wake up tomorrow morning and find their roads cleared. They would think of him, Billy Fiddle, and how he had been out all night, freezing his butt for no thanks.

It was a relief to spot the red neon arrow on the roof of the Rockeroy, aiming at the dark building underneath it and marking the end of the street. Billy rolled into the parking lot and saw a light on in one of the small windows at the back. Frank's station wagon, Oren's squad car, Sy Peske's pick-up and Jake's new Ford were parked by the side door, mounds of snow with antennas sticking out, drifts piling up to the door handles. Billy waited but no one came to the door. Maybe they had the jukebox turned up. Maybe they were down in the basement in Billy Quail's room where they couldn't hear the sound of the plow. He circled the parking lot with the blade up, put it down, and after a last look over his shoulder, started back up the street.

Lee would have gone in. He would have gone in roaring laughter, grabbing hands and slapping backs and calling everybody's name, buddy-buddy all around, everybody pushing back their chairs and jumping up to buy him a shot, making him sit down, making him stay. When Billy came in, they made room for him, too, but it was Lee they'd gathered around and looked towards, Lee they'd always told not to leave after the game broke up. Lee was the type to bend over backwards to make jackasses feel wise and liars honest, and although that had made him popular at the bar, sometimes Billy wondered if that was why everybody was trying to forget Lee now, because they knew damn well what crap they'd dumped on him at the end when he lay there in bed. Helpless to get away from it, all those stupid get-well cards and self-righteous advice and you-know-how-sick-Wackett-was-and-he-got-better stories that only made Lee feel worse. He shouldn't have let them do it. He should have let Billy throw them out, should have told them to send their pity straight to hell. Lee, not in bed with his eyes emptied out and everybody crying, but Lee on the porch, bellowing at Billy to come out and make him laugh, those two shiny green boots of his propped up on the railing, lizardskins aglow in the dark.

"That's right, all you can-openers," shouted Billy over the roar of the engine. "Go ahead and forget. It's just me out here. Me and my plow." He pressed down hard on the horn.

> *"Oh it snowed so bad the night I left,*
> *The weather it was dry*
> *I left up north to sell my whores,*
> *Suzanna, don't you cry—"*

Passing Chapel of Our Saviour, his foot on the gas and then on the brake, he slid sideways with a flourish. The edge of the blade hit a pole, a satisfying crunch. He put her in neutral and switched off the headlights. The wind cried in the dark.

He opened the Red Spot and had himself a snort. Maybe he should just park here and walk back over to the bar. There was no reason not to. Frank and the others would insist on him staying for a little comfort, at least until he had warmed up enough to make it home. Anybody would on a night like this, but especially Frank, who would think Billy had finally come in to why and cry over Lee. Frank thought Billy was still grieving. They all did. They were fools. Billy hadn't cried since the funeral and even then the tears had come more from exhaustion than anything else. Not that he didn't miss Lee. Lee had been his brother, they had slept in the same room and worn the same clothes and shared the same birthday and drunk out of the same bottle and always pulled each other out of tangles and some nights Billy got so angry about it that he wanted to take Lee and Stephy's Chevy out to the arroyo east of Stygo and sail it right off the edge. Because the truth of it was that even though they looked identical, Lee wasn't anything like Billy. Lee was just Lee, just the guy who laughed a lot and drank too hard and worried about going bald or broke or nuts along with every-body else at the Rockeroy on Friday nights. Lee was a piker, that was his problem. He was always saying he had plans for the future, but Lee's idea of plans turned out to be a splin-ter-mouthed wife, a plow he wouldn't fix, a secondhand car, and church on Sunday. Church! Oh, Lee was a good guy, for sure he'd been a good guy; he had always stuck up for his brother, that's what they all kept reminding Billy at the funeral. But Lee had had that drinking problem, which made it a good thing he'd gotten cancer because if it hadn't been cancer, which was quick and not too painful, it prob-ably would have been his liver, which according to Jake Loper was the worst way in the world to go. Instead, Lee's bones had gone bad, dusted into bone meal before anyone even caught on he was sick, first in his fingers and toes and then in his arms and legs and then everywhere at once. Billy imagined it like chalk that washed away in the blood, rock salt carried off by the river in the spring run-off. No, people cashed in every day, people with a lot more going for them than Lee had had. Everybody knew it, they just didn't think it was healthy to admit it now that Lee was gone.

Billy saw something move, someone out there, leaning against the blizzard, stumbling towards the Rockeroy. The storm howled through the crack in the windshield. He had to push against the wind to get the door open.

"Hey! Who's there?" His words flew away in the wind. He fumbled for the flashlight under the seat, turned it on and aimed it. The figure staggered as the light fell on him. He turned slowly, his hood falling back. It was Frank.

He had a rope in one hand and mittens and a bottle in the other. He started towards the plow with one arm up to see, but he slipped and fell backwards into a snow bank. Reaching over his shoulder to pull up his hood he dropped the bottle, then both mittens. He gave up on his hood and waited a moment, then heaved to his feet, picked up his things and started towards the plow again.

"What're you doing," shouted Billy.

Frank looked up, leaning against the wind. "That you, Billy?"

"No," shouted Billy. "It's the mailman."

Frank gripped his mittens to his chest, trying to stay on his feet. "I'm looking for Betsy. You didn't see her out on the highway, did you?"

Billy aimed the flashlight towards his own face. "No," he shouted against the wind. "What you got in that bottle?"

But instead of handing it over, Frank waved and turned away.

"Frank!"

He stopped and turned slowly and Billy gestured for him

to come closer. "You can't hear me over there," he shouted. He lifted an ear flap, pointing at his ear.

Frank lowered his head against the wind and struggled over to the cab, raising a hand into the beam of light to grab the bottom of the door. His face looked confused and slapped together by the cold. Billy guessed he was drunk. "I don't know how the hell I'm supposed to find her in this shit," called Frank. "I don't even know what direction she took off in."

"Hell, buddy, there is no direction tonight. They all got blown away."

Frank let go of the door and stepped back, staggering against the wind, trying to put his mittens on. "I don't know," he said. "I guess I'll keep looking." He pulled up his hood and stumbled away from the cab.

"Hey, Frank," shouted Billy.

Frank turned and cupped his hands around his mouth. "If you see her on your way home, put her next to you in the cab. She'll stay right there." He started off again.

Billy was surprised. Frank was usually so solicitous with him. He waited until the wind paused to gather for another blast. "Frank," he shouted. "You order this weather, or what? I nearly went off the road ten times trying to get here."

Frank turned and held up his hands. "Can't hear you." He started to say something else, but stopped as if it was not worth the effort, waving good-bye instead.

"Hey," shouted Billy. He had to shout a second time before Frank turned. Billy motioned him back to the cab and Frank came slowly, fighting the storm. He stopped a few steps away. "What is it?"

For lack of knowing what to say, Billy pointed at the bottle. Frank looked down at the bottle and passed it up to Billy.

"Take it," he said, looking out at the storm.

Billy aimed the light at the label. "Just what I need." He didn't like bourbon but he took a swallow. When he looked down, Frank was leaning out past the door, squinting into the wind. Billy stretched his leg out of the cab and touched Frank's chest with his boot. Frank turned with a start.

"Get a grip, Frank. It's just a dog."

"Yeah." Frank leaned into the cab so he wouldn't have to shout. "I forgot to let her in, though. I was playing poker with the boys and I started winning. I just clean forgot." He looked at Billy as if he expected some kind of answer. "Hell," he said. "What good are explanations now, right?" He peered over his shoulder at the storm. "Eleven years she's been with me. I might just as well have dropped her off in Siberia."

"Hey, listen. I'm freezing to death. What say we go over to the bar and you buy me a cup—"

Frank turned. "She's what I got, though," he burst out. "That's it, Lee. That dog's all I—" As he slipped, his hood fell back but he stayed on his feet by grabbing the bottom of the door. "Shit," he said. He leaned into the cab again. "I'm sorry, Billy. I didn't mean to call you Lee."

"No big deal. Life goes on."

"No, really. You don't have to. I'd feel the same way if I'd lost a twin brother. I guess you and him were used to it when he was alive, but it must be God awful to have it happen now that—"

Billy looked down at Frank sharply. "You need a hearing aid or something? I said it's okay."

"Aw, no it isn't." Frank looked out at the storm and

cursed, wiping the back of his fist against his mouth. "It's not okay. Nothing's okay. It's losing the dog. I'm not thinking straight." He stopped suddenly, trying to control the muscles of his face, the crack of emotion that was opening up in his voice. Billy decided to look away, staring at the front windshield. "I know it's nothing but an old dog," said Frank. "I know it."

"That's right."

But when he felt the moment had passed he looked down and saw that instead of being ashamed, Frank was angry. He slapped his hood down over his eyes and turned away. He took a step and then another, lurching sideways as the wind caught him.

Billy shouted, but something in the way Frank waved him off and kept walking made his own anger rise up. He leaned out and aimed the flashlight at Frank's back.

"Okay, Frank," he yelled. "You want some advice? I'll tell you what you do. You learn to lighten up." Frank staggered sideways and turned, holding up his hand against the light, his face wet with tears. Billy felt all of his patience leave. It was like the beginning of desire. "Think of all the dog food you'll save." He switched off the flashlight. "Think of how happy the cats will be."

Frank was back at the plow in two steps, throwing the door wide. He would have pulled Billy from the cab but Billy grabbed onto the steering wheel. They struggled and then Frank was on the running board, heaving himself up into the cab, pushing Billy against the back window.

"That dog's been with me eleven years. I don't care what you do about your own losses, but you try to laugh off me losing Betsy and I'll strangle you right—"

Billy held up a finger between them. "Hey, Frank. Aren't you forgetting something?"

Frank's whole body was shaking. "What are you talking about?"

"Aren't I the one who lost a brother?" He lifted his head, moved it an inch closer to Frank's fist. "My twin brother, Frank. Remember? The one who kicked? The one everybody loved best? Or have you already forgotten? Lee, I mean."

Frank pushed Billy away so hard his head hit the side window. "Don't you talk to me, you little greaseball," he shouted. "You don't know what love is."

Frank's nose was running. His lips were blue and the tip of his nose was white. It was easy to push him off the running board. He cried out, grabbing at air and falling backwards out of the cab, landing heavily in the snow. He struggled like a turtle on its back and then gave in and lay back. When Billy called out, Frank put his arm over his head and hid his face.

"Hey." Billy picked up the bottle of bourbon and climbed down from the cab, the wind biting into his face. "Frank?" He leaned over, set the bottle in the snow and shined the flashlight. Frank's face, or what Billy could see of it, was purple and striped in frozen white tears. "Hey old fart." He reached out to help him up but Frank jerked his arm free.

"Get away from me."

Billy stood still, trying to decide. "You can't just lie there. Come on, Frank. You're drunk, you know that? You're going to freeze to death, you know. Oren's going to have to come by with the meat wagon and carve you out." But a moan of wind blasted snow in his face and Frank did not move and all of it seemed suddenly too much to deal with. "How do you think I feel," he shouted. The words burned in his throat and flew away in a howl of wind. "I got to drive all the way home alone. You think I like this? You think I'm doing this for the fresh air? I'm probably going to get lost out there on the flats and end up frozen at the bottom of some ditch, so you might as well quit blubbering about that dead dog and start blubbering for me. You hear me, Frank?" He flicked off the flashlight and went back to the plow. He climbed in, slammed the door, and restarted the engine.

He sat with his hands in his lap, searching the crack running along the front windshield. The glass had already iced over, but from the sound outside, he guessed that the storm was starting to blow itself out. He pulled his hood up over his cap, tied the strings under his chin, turned on the lights, and wiped the windshield clear with the rag. It served Frank right to hear the truth for once. Maybe next time he wouldn't waste his breath bawling over a broken-down dog that was probably better off dead. Billy threw the rag on the floor and took out his bottle of Red Spot.

He waited for the knock on the cab but it did not come. When he opened the door Frank was gone. There was nothing in sight except the bottle of bourbon next to a sitz mark in the snow. It was hard to believe anyone had been there at all.

Billy put away his bottle and drew on his gloves. Death wasn't so bad. Maybe Frank didn't realize it yet, but it was the waiting that hurt, not death. It was the words "your brother is sick" that had made Billy feel as if his life had been built on an ocean of ice with a huge hole punched open in the center towards which everything he had ever known or loved or believed in was beginning to slide. "Lee's dead" was nothing more than a fact, a heavy plug of ice slamming down over the hole, sealing it closed with a solid and final thunk. Why, he could go anywhere now. Mexico. California. Miami. There was no need to wait for the worst to happen anymore. It already had. It was over, it was behind him, it could never be repeated. "Lee's dead," he yelled, and despite the ice in his hands and feet, a fierce white heat charged through him. It was as if he'd opened the door to a high-stoked furnace and jumped inside. He blew the horn hard and shifted into first, heading for the highway.

But he did not get far. He did not even get out to the highway. After he passed Sy Peske's shop, as he was passing the You Are Now Leaving Stygo sign, he shifted accidentally from third into first.

Again and again he tried to restart her. He cursed and begged and wiggled the gas pedal, the gear shift, the starter button, sweat breaking under his cap and trickling down his face into his eyes. The cab was filled with the smell of gas. He bellowed and banged his fist on the wheel. But there was nothing else to do. He turned off the plow to wait.

It was still snowing, but much more gently. When he pushed back his hood and lifted his ear flaps, he realized the howling had stopped. The silence outside had a thin, breakable quality to it. He leaned the back of his head against the rear window and felt his blood roaring. He was sweating, but he was very cold. He reached under the seat for the thermos of coffee and found it on its side with the top loose. The floor of the cab was wet, the boots he had tried to waterproof soaked through. He wondered if his feet were frostbitten. The line down his throat into his chest no longer burned. He unscrewed the Red Spot and drank until the bottle was empty, exhaled and then turned with a grunt and looked out the rear window.

The town was gone already, nothing left of it but the red neon arrow poised above the Rockeroy, blushing in the dark. Out each side window only dark, huddled shapes under blankets of snow, and up ahead nothing at all but a faint trace of the road he had cleared less than an hour before. Frank would be at home by now, waiting for his dog, maybe with the lights off so no one would see, crying over his life. Billy pictured the men at the bar, drinking and playing cards and waiting for Frank to come back, and then he pictured the things at home waiting for him. The two chairs in the kitchen by the window, the overhead light, the tap left dripping. He opened the door, leaned out and hurled the bottle backwards. It fell without a sound into the snow bank. He started to close the door when he saw a slow-moving shape.

He hung out the door. The shape was dragging towards him in the snowplow's tracks, over the snow bank to the far side of the plow where Billy could not see, a dark stain in the snow trailing behind it.

"Hey!" shouted Billy. "Who's there?"

His heart quit, then pounded to catch up with itself and he reeled back into the cab, pulling the door shut after him. What if he had hit someone? What if they were hurt, even dying, what if they expected him to take them to the hospital, see all those nurses, all those metal tables and chairs, all those hallways and rooms full of blood? He fumbled at the choke trying to get the engine to start, he could never go back there, never go through it again, but when he looked up ahead, he saw Frank's dog crawling into the headlights, dragging a piece of rope tied around her neck. She looked over her shoulder into the headlights, crumpled hind legs shivering, her whole body matted in ice. "*Lee's dead!*" Billy shouted, sucking in air and hitting the horn as hard as he could. Betsy wagged her tail uncertainly and crippled across the road and down into the irrigation ditch.

Billy opened the door, tear-blinded by the sudden cold, and jumped from the cab into the snow bank. Trying to get around the plow he stumbled and caught himself on the blade. He took two high-kneed steps through the drift and felt himself beginning to slip, the lizardskin boots as useless for traction as they were for warmth. He slid into the ditch on all fours, calling the dog.

He would take her back to Frank. They would dry her off and light a fire for her. They would sit down and make a toast to her, just the two of them, talk about how lucky Frank was. But Billy would not stay long. He would stay long enough to make sure things were all right and then he would put on his sweaters and gloves and boots and walk back out to his plow. Oh yes, long before the storm died out, long before dawn, long before anyone else woke up. He had forgotten to mark the fenceline the way Lee had warned him to so that he could spot it in the dark and follow it to his driveway, but he was not afraid of missing the turn-off. He would find his way back the same way this dog had found him: by instinct, by feel, by the need for human comfort—all those stubborn, unconvinced threads of memory that survivors have to count on, pulling Billy through the dark towards home.

NINE

DANCING WITH WILLA

DANCING
WITH WILLA

Just before sunset, which for Frank Stiles was not when the winds started lying down or when the Red Spot whistles blew, but when the west-reflecting corner window on the second floor of the old hotel across the street turned from a blank to a gold so fierce he could not stare directly at it, the radio reported that the swarm had changed course. Frank called the bar to tell Billy Quail and the cafe to tell Caroline Potts, and then with a last, resigned glance toward the hotel, he went downstairs, closed the filling station, and drove out to the fields to tell the pickers.

The swarm had mowed through the northern part of the county in two days, but out on the salt flats where nothing grew, it had hesitated and spread out, just enough to give rise to the hope that this time Stygo was going to be in luck. But that was before a light breeze from the northeast had started, just like everyone in Stygo over the age of fifty predicted, a breeze sweet with the smell of Stygo's ripening sugar beets. Tomorrow morning, the farm report said, afternoon at the latest. That is, Frank reminded the workers, unless the wind shifted—which, of course, was impossible, since in June the wind never shifted, at least not in any June Stygo could remember, not when a swarm was about to hit. The younger

men threw down their tools and cursed the horizon or the dirt or the measly little beets that had only begun to grow; but those not so young, those who knew by now it was always the hole between wishing you were safe and knowing you never would be that tripped you up, didn't bother. Faith is for fools, they said, and with their hands in their pockets, they walked back to Stygo.

But they did not change their clothes when they got home, or fetch their mail or feed their animals or make their dinners or stop at the bar. They boarded up their windows and stuffed rags up their chimneys and then they took their smudge pots and blankets and brooms and rags and anybody strong enough to use them and straggled back out to the fields. In ditches bordering the sugar beets they set up old sheepherder tents, and after pooling supplies they went back to work. It was that simple. So that by midnight when they showed up at the cook tent one by one, they weren't talking beets or blisters or swarms anymore. They'd forgotten about paychecks and clean clothes and bumper crops and better tools. They sat on the ground and ate, and when the food was gone they went back to work. No longer waiting for their dreams to rise or their work to end, no longer waiting for the beets to grow, no longer waiting for anything at all but the swarm; and when Frank's station wagon filled with Red Spot rum rolled up to the edge of the field, though no one stopped picking, they got drunk while they worked and forgot even the swarm. They turned off their minds and picked until their hands were bleeding, until they were only a small swarm themselves, until they couldn't even remember why they were there or why the swarm was hitting early or what they had ever wanted in the first place, until by dawn of the next day they'd forgotten everything they had ever wished or hoped or waited for except sleep.

Which meant, of course, they'd forgotten Willa Moon.

Willa Moon, who had shown up a year ago out of nowhere, stepping off the Greyhound as if she owned the place and moving into the abandoned Stygo Grand, living there now with a set of keys to every room and the windows open so that birds flew in and out. The always swearing and laughing and half-crazy and wanting to dance because she was always drunk Willa Moon. Asleep now, unknowing now, somewhere deep inside that rotting carcass of a hotel. Maybe she lay on the floor outside the numbered rooms, still dressed and dreaming off last night's tequila while the pickers out in the fields worked and dreamed off her. Maybe down in the lobby, keeled over like a picket fence before a headwind, or maybe on one of the beds, lying there now, slack-mouthed, wrapped in a piece of curtain. Willa Moon, Willa Moon, the men whispered—and then forgot, along with everything else, because Willa Moon knew nothing of work and sacrifice and what it is to wait. Willa Moon asleep now, dreaming now, knowing nothing and caring nothing about knowing at all.

■

It was dark by the time Frank was able to get back upstairs to call his sister. Pearl had been laid up all week with the flu and was not used to being alone in her house and after he told her that a swarm was expected in tomorrow, for several minutes he could not get a word in. "Yes," he said, squeezing the bone between his eyes. "I know. I'll be there as soon as I can. Just do the best you can. Cover it with a blanket then. Yes, I'll nail it shut. I know, Pearl. I promise, yes."

After he hung up, he put a bowl of food in front of his dog, Betsy, and went downstairs to lock the gas pump. The street was dusty, the air soft and still. The only car was his own, parked down the street in front of the Sugar Beet. He went around back and stuffed oil rags under the back door, stuffed more rags into the air conditioner vents and propped a piece of cardboard over the cracked window, holding it in place with a two-by-four. He went back inside and plugged the drain in the restroom with paper towels, and then after a last look toward the hotel, he closed up and walked down to the Rockeroy. On a normal night he would have been elbow-deep in bartending by now. But no one would be coming in tonight, not until it was over.

On the porch, he smelled corn and molasses. Letting himself in, he banged the screen door behind him to let Billy Quail know he was there. He could feel Billy's daughter watching from a booth at the back of the room, but he did not turn around. Despite being Yiwa, Kwami had been at one point in his life a source of painfully impossible daydreams, even fantasies, a girl pretty enough to make him speechless if she had so much as glanced his way. But that was before she had fallen off the bridge south of town. Now she was ruined and always would be, the diamond-shaped face turned flat, with big, black, emptied-out eyes and a sharp little hook of a mouth always stained brown with molasses. Now all she could do was stare and eat candy.

Frank took two beers out of the cooler, opened them and set one on the service window for Billy. "Any problems, Geronimo?" He leaned around the service window to the fuse box to turn on the neon arrow up on the roof. "Everything set?"

Billy shrugged. He stood at the grill, a small, bitter-mouthed Yiwa with skin the texture of parchment. He was stirring something, one hand on his hip. From the looks of his apron, he'd been at it all day.

"I think we're really in for it this time." Frank pulled a stool up next to the service window. "You been out in the last hour? Feels like a bomb's set to go off."

"All I have is corn," said Billy. "They took the chili I made out to the pickers."

"That's all right." Frank took a swig and belched. "I like corn." He heard a squeak from the booth behind him and he opened the till, making himself busy counting the day's take. Pearl and Johanna had nicknamed Kwami the Praying Mantis. The wetbacks said she carried bad luck. Frank didn't believe it—Kwami was just Kwami, it was just the way things had turned out for her. Her staring was just something to get used to, like everything else. But on a night like tonight, with the town so empty and quiet, it was irritating. He heard her skin stick to and squeak against the vinyl seat. When she started making sucking noises on the candy stick, he put away the money and leaned in the service window.

"Bill? I'm going to switch the station. I been listening to farm reports all day."

He reached for the radio under the sill and hit Roy Orbison in Kansas City. He turned it up and dropped back into his seat, nodding to the rhythm. He unfolded his penknife to work on his nails. After a while, he put his knife away, took another swallow of beer, got up again and turned down the radio. "Hey, Geronimo," he called. "You trying to get your daughter's teeth to fall out from sugar rot or what."

The fan in the kitchen clicked off and Billy came out with

two plates and a bowl of corn on the cob. He shouted at Kwami in Yiwa, harsh sounds like a drawer of silverware dumped on the floor, and she dropped the stick of molasses candy as if he'd swatted it from her mouth. When he motioned with his head, she skittered out of the booth and fled down the back stairs. Billy nudged shut the door of the cellar, set dinner on the counter, and pulled up a stool beside Frank.

"Sorry, Frank."

"It's okay."

Frank liked Billy Quail because for a Yiwa he worked hard and didn't complain about things you couldn't change like weather or swarms or old age or females. Over the years they'd arrived at an understanding about this, and other things. Frank never let anyone in the bar joke about Kwami, and in turn, Billy didn't listen to the things people said about Frank's shyness around women or his ignorance of beet farming. Frank picked out an ear of corn and salted it. "Anybody stop in this afternoon?"

"Liz Loper for a while. That's all." Billy set an ear of corn on end and began sawing at it with his knife. "The bosses took my chili to the pickers. Didn't even ask. I was over helping Harley cover his Camaro. When I got back there was a note saying put it on the company tab."

"Assholes." Frank gnawed his corn until his mouth was full, took a swig of beer, glanced at Billy out of the corner of his eye and then swallowed and asked casually, "Think Willa Moon'll come by?"

"No."

They ate in silence, side by side, their eyes fixed on the opposite wall. When they were done, Billy wiped down the counter and took the plates to the kitchen. Frank waited a moment and then heaved to his feet and went through the saloon doors to the back barroom.

The air was beery and stale from the night before. He lifted a mouse from the cage above the cash register behind the bar and dropped it in Shirley's cage. According to the Coors clock, it was 8:15. On any other night the booths would be full, the jukebox playing, everybody shouting for drinks. But not tonight. Tonight nothing would happen. Not until after the swarm was over, and then they would come all at once, all of them loud and filthy and pissed off by loss, beating down the doors for a drink, howling for a fight and looking for Willa Moon.

All day he had told himself to go home after dinner, try for a good night's rest. He leaned against the bar, picking his teeth with a match and contemplating the snake and the mouse. Shirley never killed anything while she was being watched. The mouse sprang over her coils and rose on its hind legs, sniffing the air. Frank thought about Kwami downstairs, her eyes on the ceiling, listening to the footsteps overhead, waiting for his to go away so that Billy would let her come up. He dragged his stool across the floor and coughed, opening a seed catalog Sam Waters had left the night before. Billy came in with a can of tobacco, took off his apron and sat opposite him to roll a cigarette.

"She's probably gone," he said, striking a match.

Frank did not look up. "Who."

"Who we're waiting for. She's probably already halfway to somewhere else by now."

But Billy was wrong. At nine sharp, the door out in the front room banged and high heels clicked across the threshold. Waiting for the smell of her, Frank leaned over his reading so Billy would not see his face. Kwami smelled like molasses candy, and his sister smelled like the inside of an old bottle on a hot day. But Willa Moon was another matter. Pearl liked to say it was only perfume, but Frank knew no bottle in the world could hold such a smell. Even when the bar was packed with workers pushing around her for a dance, the smell was still there, a smell that could make Frank feel as excited and ashamed as if he'd been caught spying on her naked. Tonight, waiting for the force of it to hit him was enough to shake him into almost wishing he'd gone home instead. The click of high heels stopped, the saloon doors cried open and Willa Moon cleared her throat, waiting for them to look up.

Tonight she was wearing the red dress and she should have been wearing a slip. She had her black hair loose, with eyes shot bluer than ever, the look of someone who has achieved blindness by an act of will and means to keep it. She laughed, tossing back her head so they could see her throat, but when she realized no one else was there, she stopped.

"Jesus. You're going to tell me they're out there working. Aren't you?"

A shiver of panic went through Frank. "It'll be over tomorrow. The radio says the swarm's coming through tomorrow."

"Tomorrow?" Willa narrowed her eyes. "And when is that?"

He felt his face heat up. "You mean when tomorrow? Dawn. Probably just before—"

"Dawn." Willa spat it off her tongue and dropped it. "Well, then. We got ourselves a problem, boys." She came towards them in slow motion, jutting her hips, leaning in, eyes half-mast, closing out the room and everything in it. "It's tonight." Her hand hit the bar hard enough to make Billy's ashtray jump. "And tonight Willa doesn't give a rat's ass about bugs."

Billy muttered something in Yiwa but Frank couldn't breathe. All summer long he had waited for his chance with Willa Moon—he had prayed for it, for God's sake—and now here they were and nobody to stop him, all he knew was that he had nothing to say and never had and that the only thing he wanted now was her to leave, to disappear, to at least turn her back on him out of mercy . . . but he could not finish the thought. She was turning her back, slowly, the way a cat might turn its back on a pack of fenced-in dogs. Frank felt seasick watching her leave, the red dress slit low in back and attached to her hips like a second skin. Yet when she paused at the doorway, turning one last time, as she always did before she left, she looked a little pale and wide-eyed herself. "For Christ's sake," she cried. "What is wrong with this town?" And was gone, the saloon doors batting at air.

Billy dumped his ashtray, wiped it with a rag, and put it behind the bar. He unplugged the jukebox light and paused at the door to the kitchen. "You staying or you want me to close up?"

Frank wanted to stay. He wanted to breathe that smell down over him again, take back the scene and make it over. He turned to tell Billy to go on but then he realized another smell in the room. The much stronger, brown smell of molasses. The room was dark and still but he knew. By the door, in the one booth where Billy and Frank would not see her but where Willa would have to, sucking a molasses angel cane, her eyes round and black and empty. He looked in that direction and a head rose up over the top of a booth. Staring like something that never slept, something that didn't know what sleep was anymore and didn't care.

"Never mind," he said to Billy. "I promised Pearl I'd drop by." He picked up the catalog and threw it in the trash. Billy went out to the front room, calling down in the cellar for Kwami to help him close. She did not move or make a sound and for a moment Frank felt his anger rise against her. But he had shouted at her once before for bothering Willa Moon and for three days afterwards paid for it: sucked-over stubs of molasses candy suddenly everywhere he looked, stuck to the back of his shirt, under his bar rag, in his wallet, under his desk at the station, behind the money in the till, in Betsy's fur, even at Pearl's house, under his pillow. He didn't know how she did it without being seen or what it meant, but it gave him the creeps, and that he didn't need, not tonight with the streets so still with waiting. "Go help Billy," he said and though she did not move, he turned off the light above Shirley's bowl, unplugged the juke, and went out the back way through the kitchen.

He stood on the porch, facing away from the town. There was no moon yet and the stars were thick, the land stretching out under them as flat and black as a pool of tar. He found it odd that the fields at night looked just the same covered by beets as they had looked in his father's time covered by range grass and sheep. In daylight things changed, for better or worse; but at night it all looked the same, the same as it had looked for a thousand years, and the same as it might look in a thousand more.

He looked south in the direction of Pearl's house, thinking that was where he should be now. Yet when he stepped off the porch and circled round to the front of the building, he headed north. He had to pass the side window of the Rockeroy and did so quickly, ignoring the thin silhouette watching him from inside, fingers spread against the glass.

The night air in the street had a dream-like, etherized quality to it. Even the neon buzz of the arrow on top of the Rockeroy seemed muted. Something was coming all right, maybe worse than the last time. At the hotel, Willa Moon's window, at least the window of the room he believed she stayed in more than the others, was open and the shade was up, but the light was not on.

He pulled the rags out from the door of the filling station and let himself in. Betsy, who could barely move for her arthritis anymore, groaned and thumped her tail in greeting. He sat down at his desk in the dark, feeling in the bottom drawer for the bottle of Red Spot rum. If he slumped to one side, he could have watched the window of the hotel across the street without being seen. But tonight he did not. Tonight he sat up straight and stared at the door in the dark, angry, and getting angrier.

It was not just the coming swarm, not just the empty streets and the tension building and Kwami sneaking around after him. He was used to all that. He'd been through it before. That was just the way it was sometimes. No, what had got under his skin was Willa Moon sashaying over to the bar like that as if she didn't care that the swarm was coming, as if she hadn't even heard yet, or as if it didn't matter. All she cared about was having a roomful of men get stupid over her and buy her drinks and wait for a dance with her. And now she'd be back in the hotel, drinking and thinking what-ever she thought about while Frank would be across the street, waiting just like always for the swarm to get here, only this year he'd be drinking and thinking about her. He closed his eyes and for a moment wanted to agree with everything Pearl and Johanna said about Willa Moon. Sure, she was beautiful. Sure, he liked to watch. But what good was beauty if all it did in the end was to make a man hate his life and everything in it?

Something made of glass smashed the outside of the front door. Betsy scrambled to her feet and began barking at the wall. Frank jerked out of his chair and threw his cap. Goddammit, somebody had to look after the town while they were out in the fields, why couldn't the pickers get that straight? Maybe he didn't have the calluses to prove it, but his job wasn't all that easy. "What," he shouted at the door. "You think I like twiddling my thumbs all night? You think I wouldn't rather be dead?"

It felt good to shout, like something he'd saved for all month. "Shut the hell up!" he yelled. Betsy quit barking as if she'd been yanked off her feet by a rope. Frank scooped up his cap, opened the front door and stepped out on the porch.

The moon was up, a fat, fake-looking moon that lit up the street like a stage. There was no one in sight. The Rockeroy's arrow glowed up at one end of town, and down at the other, a single streetlight at the highway turn-off. Peaceful as a ghost town, he thought.

But when he looked down he saw a spark in the weeds beside the stoop. It was a piece of wet glass, and turning it in his hand, he noticed other pieces spattered out into the street; and then suddenly, maybe because he was tired or because the street was so quiet and waitful, time turned back to the night on the bridge so many years ago, only this time it was not Kwami who everyone had given up for lost, it was Frank. He was lying on his back at the bottom of the ditch, he was looking up through the water to the steel girders on the underside of the bridge and the row of scared faces peering over the rail, but beyond that, he was looking to the moon. He'd fallen out of the world, been dropped like a stone, yet all the while, as if none of it mattered, the moon was keeping watch on the surface of the water, spattering into little pieces of broken glass, sealing him in underneath.

Frank blinked his eyes. Kwami was the one who had fallen. She was the one who hadn't cared. When Jack told her what they were going to do, when he told her, overdoing it as he always did when he had a bad idea, that the only way out was to beg for mercy, she had laughed harder than any of them. Jack was the one who let go of her wrist, but he and Sy still had her other wrist and when Frank shouted that he and Sam and Oren had her, too, that they wouldn't let go, that she wouldn't fall, couldn't ever, she had giggled instead and twisted her other wrist free, making them all shout with fear as she flopped upside down, held by her ankles, dangling over the swollen black water below, her underpants glowing even whiter in the dark than her pale canestalk legs. With his thumb and first finger Frank pressed his eyes closed. What had she wanted back then? What had any of them wanted? He pressed until the back of his skull lit up and when it occurred to him that what he was smelling was not the ditch water but mescal, he heard a voice.

"Hey. Look up."

He opened his eyes—not to the dark underbelly of the

bridge but to the dusty hotel lobby across the street and above that, leaning out the window on the second floor as if he'd dreamed her there, the silhouette of Willa Moon. She'd taken off the bug screen and her hair hid her face from the bare light in the room behind her. Frank forgot everything.

"A bottle rocket from the moon." Laughter like bright-colored silk floated down into the street. "That's what this town needs tonight. Fireworks." Set against the dark tangle of hair, her throat glowed white. "Howlers." She looked down at him, folded her arms and leaned against the side of the window. "So," she said, pointing to the station behind him. "Neighbor. What do you do over there all day long. You ever spy on me?"

"Oh God, no," said Frank, nearly choking. "Me?" He tried to laugh. He looked down the street, rubbing the back of his neck, trying to relax his breathing.

"I would," she said. "Cures boredom. You been living there all this time?"

"I moved there last winter. I was living with my sister at her house but—she's kind of the sensitive type. I thought it best I got my own place."

"From what I remember, Pearl's not so sensitive. I hear since she started drinking, she's gotten pretty long claws."

He shrugged and looked away. Pearl was all right. She just didn't relate to women like Willa Moon.

He looked up. She was standing straight, leaning back now. The light behind her was shining through her hair, shining as if she was on fire.

"Tell me, Frank. You must know this place pretty well. What do you think the problem is?"

He scratched his elbow and looked down the street.

"Well, for one thing," he tried, "there's no taxi service."

Her laughter made his heart want to jump up and salute. "No," she said. "I mean the men in this town. Tonight." She dropped from view and re-emerged with a bottle in her hand. She opened it and took a slow swallow. "Where is everybody?"

Frank felt his heart fall. But what had he expected? Even at his best, he didn't have the looks of a Jake Loper or the moves of a Harley Barrows or the money of an Oren Whatly, and he'd never been much at telling jokes. The best he had to offer was that he was nice. Everybody said he was nice. But for someone like Willa Moon who had seen so much of the world, what did nice add up to? He looked up at her window.

"They'll be back. They have to wait for the swarm to get here. That's all. It's just the way things are."

She leaned forward, resting her chin in her hands. "That's why they're crazy?"

Frank looked up. "I didn't say—"

"Yes you did." Her voice was lazy, drifting. "And you're right. They're out there in the fields, crazy as shithouse rats, waiting for a bunch of bugs to come and ruin everything. They've been waiting for it all summer. In fact, if that swarm doesn't get here tonight, I'll bet they all just drop on their knees out there and start crying, 'What'd we do wrong, God?'" She rocked forward, laughter spilling through her voice. "I asked your brother in Sweetwater about it, you know," she said. "I said, Jack, what if after tonight you didn't have anything bad left to wait for? What if only good things could happen to you? And you know what Jack said? He goes, 'Why don't you shut up for once, Willa Moon?

Everybody in town thinks you're nuts.'"

Frank felt himself redden. "Jack isn't much on manners. Besides, nobody in Stygo would ever—"

"It's okay, Frank. It's their problem, not mine." She looked away, lifted one arm and swept a wide arc outside the window. "You know what?" she said. "The really sad part is that they've got nothing in it anymore." She looked down at him. "You know what I mean," she said. "Faith. In things being fun anymore."

She studied him a long moment and then closed her eyes and took a drink. Frank waited, looking up, wondering what it would feel like to put your hand on a throat as white as that. She leaned forward to wipe her bottom lip with the heel of her hand and then stopped, lowering her hand slowly, staring down the street at the Rockeroy arrow. A moment later she looked down at Frank. "You remember what fun is," she said. "Don't you?"

The way she leaned out the window a little and looked straight down into him—he couldn't help it. He felt his heart speed up, felt his cheeks turn warm. He took off his cap. "I hope so," he said. "I've always hoped so."

But now she was staring up the street, out at the dark beyond the town again. "It's not just tonight, you know," she said. "It's every night. It's all their lives. I tell them, Don't you try and make me crazy with those bug stories of yours. Don't you dare. But still I can feel them thinking it, even when they promise they're not." She bent out of the window, farther this time. Her hair fell forward over her shoulders. "That's the joke of it," she laughed. "Because if all people ever do around here is wait for the bugs to come, then the bugs just have to keep coming. They have to.

Because nobody believes in anything else anymore."

Frank stopped listening. As she went on, she began leaning farther out over the sill, pressing her words at him, leaning so far out that she looked as if she might snap off at the waist any minute. Frank stared up, nodding, wondering what it might be like to catch half of her in his arms.

"What's the matter? Why are you looking at me like that?"

"I wasn't looking—"

She straightened up. "You think I'm making this up? You think I'm kidding?"

"No, I—"

"If you don't believe me, then what about the way they hold me when we dance? They don't hold me like men anymore. They hold me like kids afraid of the dark. Tell me," she cried, slapping the outside of the building. "What do they want?"

"I—maybe I never thought about it." He looked down the street and ran his hand through his hair, feeling as if there was another Frank Stiles standing behind the Live Bait sign, pointing at him and laughing. "I don't know, Miss Moon. I guess I try not to—"

"You don't know? Then how come you're not out there in the fields, whying and dying about tomorrow with the rest of them? Or home with that boa constrictor sister of yours? How come you spent all your money putting a big red arrow on the roof of that old bar of yours?" Frank started to speak but she cut him off. "I'll tell you why. Because you're different. Because, Mr. Nice Guy, you don't give one goddamn about sugar beets and crop eaters and farm reports and never have, that's why."

Frank felt himself tighten. "Maybe you think that because I don't work in the fields I don't care. A lot of people think that. They say I have it easy. But who looks after their town till they get back? I don't get paid for it. I don't even get thanks half the time. No overtime for listening to farm reports, either. Nothing for driving back and forth relaying messages all day. And who listens to them when they come back? Who's there if it's not me?" He held up his hands. "Miss Moon, in a place like this, somebody has to hold things together—"

"Brother, I *know* what you mean." She leaned her elbows on the sill. "I mean, who is really the loony around here— that girl in the bar they hate so much? Pah-*leeze*." When Frank did not laugh, she went on. "You know the one I mean, don't you? That Yiwa who's always staring. It's not just because she fell off some bridge and hit her head a long time ago. Is it."

It was not a question. Frank shivered, feeling the blood drain out of his ears. She'd probably finished the whole pint of mescal before throwing it. She probably didn't even know what she was saying anymore. He cleared his throat.

"Say what, now?"

She was leaning back to drink, but she stopped. She lowered the bottle and then pointed at him.

"Come here. Come closer to the window. You can't hear me over there."

He swallowed hard and looked down the street. Why had he ever wished for anything? He hooked his fingers in his front pockets and stepped forward. She leaned past the window sill so that her hair slid forward, hiding her face from the moon.

"Know what I think?" she said. "I think if you ever got the chance to ask that Yiwa what emptied out her eyes, she'd lean over and whisper: 'This place did.'" Willa pulled her lips back so that he could see most of her teeth. "Didn't it, Frank."

He turned and looked at the red arrow on the roof of the Rockeroy. The arrow was bright and flickering at the point, but all he could see in the dark was a little brown-stained hook of a mouth and two eyes, eyes that made her look older than her father, older than anyone else in town because they showed no memory and no forgetting, either. He closed his eyes. There was only one word for Willa Moon. She hid it pretty well, but he was no fool. Willa Moon was a tramp. A drunken tramp who didn't know a thing about life. Tonight with all this trouble on the way, he wanted to shout it in her face. He looked up and spoke carefully. "Not sure just what you mean, Miss Moon."

She looked for a moment as if he'd slapped her and then she threw back her hair to laugh. "You don't know anything about this town, right? It's not your business to know, right? You just live here."

She stopped laughing when he turned away from the window. "Hey," she called. "I don't want you to go away mad. Wait. I got something to tell you. Guess what."

But he did not want to guess what. He wanted to go home. He wanted to get his bottle of Red Spot and go upstairs, shut out the lights, switch on the television and get in bed. Betsy was whining and he went to let her out for a piss. Pearl was right. What did Willa Moon know about this town anyway? What did she care? Willa Moon. Swacked out of her mind—

"Where are you going?" Her voice sounded frightened. "You're not leaving, are you? . . . Hey. . . . I said, *Hey* . . . Frank!" And not a yard away against the Live Bait sign, a second bottle exploded, shattering into the street.

When he turned, she was standing erect so that the upper window was between them, holding herself as if she was cold. "*Gracias*." She took a small bow. "I'm not the one who's nuts, you know. I'm not. I'm just saying it's not polite to walk away when a person's talking." But she suddenly stepped back, her mouth twisting apart. She brushed at the air in front of her and then without warning, covered her eyes and began to weep.

Frank held up his hands. "I'm sorry."

"No you're not," or something like that behind her hands. "You don't understand."

"Yes I do." The truth of it was like a slap. He took a step back, trying to recover. "I'll go get you something. From the bar. Some mescal."

Willa lowered her hands. "What are you talking about?" She wiped her face roughly with the back of her hands. "You think I cry because I'm—I'm thirsty?"

"No, I just—"

"What is with this town?" she cried, flinging out her hands. "Everything I do scares you people to death. Haven't you ever cried before? Haven't you ever felt lonesome? Why do you have to do this to me?" She turned off the light in her room and reached up for the shade pull, her arm glowing white as it stretched over her head, and for a moment, only a moment, Frank saw Kwami swing off over the water, thin and pale as a wishbone in the dark. But then it was over, the shade was down and he heard Willa crying again, softer this time.

He shut his eyes, gripping his cap and feeling as if he was slipping off the edge of a cliff. "Are you all right?" His breathing echoed against the dust-softened hotel. "Willa?" The second time he said it, the crying stopped and the shade rose slowly. She was standing far enough back from the window that he could barely make her out in the darkness of her room.

"What do you want?"

What did Frank want? He wanted to leave. He wanted to leave more than he had ever wanted anything before. He could not move. What did he want? It made no sense. He held up his hands. "Would you dance with me?"

She was looking at him. "You mean at the bar?"

"I believed you," he said, and hearing it from his own mouth, he felt nearly out of his mind with belief. "I believe everything you said. Willa? I don't want to talk about swarms or droughts or—anything. I never did. All I want to do is have one dance with you. That's all."

"That's all?" But when she saw him shudder she added: "All right. Okay. Just don't make a federal case out of it. You look stupid that way."

"Willa?"

"Mmm?" And suddenly her voice changed back, softening, colors shifting through it like silk. "Go away now, sugar." She pulled the shade.

Frank waited a moment and then walked quickly, furiously to the station. As he opened the door he saw a thin shadow slip into the alley down the street. But what did Kwami matter now? What was wrong with Kwami was wrong with the whole town, Kwami just had it worse. And Frank? Frank had just been lonely. Lonely maybe all his life and afraid of getting lonelier. But now he didn't care about the fear, did-n't care about where it led a man in the end. He was done with all that. Willa had cut the heart out of it. He looked up at the moon, tilted back his head and howled. She would come to just below his chin when they danced. He pushed Betsy out the door to pee, flicked on the light, and bound-ed upstairs, yanking off his shirt as he went.

The shirt he wanted was not in his closet. After a frantic search he found it—still in its box—on top of the television under a pile of dirty work clothes. He shook it out and put it on, wondering if he remembered how to dance, kicking aside a frying pan left on the floor for Betsy, trying to see in the piece of mirror over the sink. The phone rang but since he knew it was Pearl, he didn't answer. "Hang in there, sis," he said, wiping his face on an old T-shirt. "Your brother's got things to do."

But he stopped in the stairwell, his head reeling. What if, God help him, things went so smoothly Willa would want to see the apartment? He hurried back upstairs, shoveling everything in his path into the closet. But in the end it was too much—there was still the grayness of everything and the dusty smell of farts in the couch where Betsy slept and worst of all, the tell-tale food stains on the linoleum beneath the window in the bedroom where he had eaten most of his meals, watching the hotel, spying—and in a wild panic that he was late, he flipped the lock on the apartment door, slapped it shut and thundered downstairs. He had no key, but he could sleep at Pearl's if he had to and in the morning take the door off its hinges.

When he got to the bar he was dismayed to see Billy and Kwami were still up. They were in the front room in their pajamas—Billy mixing Kwami's sedative in the blender and Kwami sitting on a beet crate next to the telephone, looking as if she'd never left. When she saw Frank open the door, she squeaked in the back of her throat and grabbed her nightgown in both fists.

"You know, I been thinking, Geronimo," shouted Frank above the noise of the blender. "If you want to take some Red Spot out to the fields in my station wagon, we can make up the lost business tonight."

Billy put down the can of lecithin and shut off the blender. He took off his glasses and looked at Frank.

"Say what now?"

Frank pulled the keys to the station wagon out of his pocket. "Booze delivery—an idea, huh? I'll stick around here, look after things while you're gone. Besides, who can sleep tonight, right?"

Billy's eyes narrowed. "I can."

Frank glanced up at the clock. "I'm trying not to be the hardnose here, okay? It's just good business. That's what we do, right? It's our job."

Billy was scrutinizing the new shirt, the way Frank had his hair. "You know as well as I do they won't let Kwami out in the fields tonight. They think she brings bad luck."

"Fine," grinned Frank. "I need the company. It's going to be a slow night."

Billy pursed his lips. He poured a thin yellow milk from the blender into a glass and handed it to Kwami, and then took his sweater down from its peg and pulled it on over his pajamas. "I don't know what's going on here. I'm not going

to ask, either. That's what you hired me for."

"Don't talk crazy. Course I'm all right."

After Billy left, Frank turned to Kwami. "What are *you* looking at?" She backed off her crate, slid along the wall and then made a dash for the cellar, clutching her head, her mouth open. Frank shut the door after her and looked at the clock. Then he went in the back bar and hid the yellow tea rose he'd swiped from Mama Jewell's garden behind the shot glasses.

He made himself a husky Red Spot and Coke and set to work. A bottle of mescal on ice, a few of the booth lights on, a rag to get the dust off the mirror behind the bar, a handful of dimes handy in the ashtray on the shelf next to the jukebox. He sat down in the middle booth to see how she would see the room, then got up to change the lights a little. Because Shirley, the snake, was in the process of swallowing her dinner, he moved her cage into the kitchen. When he came back out he noticed one of the saloon doors moving and the faint scent of molasses candy in the room. Controlling his temper, he turned away. It was too much to think about now. He would save his energy. He put some dimes in the jukebox, chose the music and sat down behind the bar with a fresh drink, all five of his senses tuned and ready.

But Willa Moon did not come.

■

By 10:00, when Frank heard Betsy whining at the back door in the kitchen and rose to let her in, he realized he was feeling the liquor, and by 10:30 he'd had another drink and the jukebox had stopped. As the silence in the room drifted in around him, he knew absolutely that Willa Moon had left town. He couldn't feel her there anymore, not the way he had felt her all summer long. She'd headed off across the fields, he could see her in his mind's eye, stumbling toward Route 286 in those high heels of hers, the moonlight on her dress. He tried to push the thought away—it was early yet, he had to be patient. He decided he could give her until midnight. But midnight came and went and after another drink, convinced that Willa Moon was gone forever, he downed his last swallow to her, went back into the kitchen and dropped the yellow tea rose in Shirley's cage.

And when he came out, mixed in with the tang of molasses, the smell he'd been waiting for hit with a force nearly strong enough to bring him to his knees. There she was, like a dream at the juke, in blue, bent over with her backside cocked at an angle. She was wearing the stockings with black lines up the backs. Frankie Lyman began to sing and she came over to the bar, snapping her fingers and looking vaguely pleased. Frank felt like God.

"Mescal." Like fur rubbing fur, the voice she used when she was ready to dance, the one she used on the pickers. Frank felt his heart swell against his chest. Almost without knowing it, he went behind the bar, fixed her drink and offered it on a napkin.

But she wasn't watching. With eyes heavy and glassed-in and bluer than ever, she was staring slack-mouthed at the booth in the corner where Kwami sat, staring as if sorting through drawers in her head and not finding what it was she was looking for. Frank dropped his ice scoop in the sink. He would tell Kwami to leave him alone, he would tell her to give up trying to ruin his life—but what he saw nearly stopped his heart. She was there all right, against the wall in the corner booth, but she was not even looking at him. She was staring at Willa, her black, emptied-out eyes wide in the dark, fascinated, the stick of candy in her mouth forgotten. He walked to the end of the bar. "Hey," he said sharply. "You go to bed!" Kwami opened her mouth and made a mewing sound but she did not look at him. He waited for her to scramble out of the booth but she did not do that, either. He looked down the bar at Willa Moon. Her face had lost color. She looked as if she might faint. He moved closer to her, pushed her drink to the edge of the bar, put out his hand and touched the blue satin. "Willa," he said loudly. "Your drink."

"Yass." She turned her body first and then her head. Holding onto the bar, she downed the drink with her eyes closed. The corner of her mouth was wet. He lifted the bottle, but she shivered and floated away and in the middle of the floor, holding the empty glass out and drifting to one side a little, she began to dance.

Frank watched for a moment and then he took a shot glass, poured two fingers of mescal and slammed it. The blood sang in his head. For a moment he could not breathe. He opened his eyes. No doubt about it. Willa Moon could dance.

But then he heard the vinyl booth squeak and the sound of teeth crunching candy like glass, and Frank turned, thinking how painless to walk over there and tear the head off that dark yellow canestalk neck of hers, as quick and painless as twisting the head off a grasshopper. He slapped down his bar rag—he was going to do something—but then he was there at the bridge again looking down over the railing and thinking he was going to be sick because he'd had too much to drink and because she was hanging upside down, not frightened at all, pushing away the curtain of her dress when it covered her face to show them, mouth open and eyes wide, grinning upside down like a fish or something not human. "Too late," she hissed when they panicked and tried to pull her back up over the railing, "too late" she shrieked and clawed for his hands, not to make him hold on and pull her back over the rail to safety, but to make him let her go. He remembered that quiet after she hit the water and disappeared, how soft and deep it was as he and the others waited at the railing, holding their breaths, knowing their lives were at the edge of never being the same again, and yet all the while, the moon on the surface of the water below so peaceful and still that when it got unbearable they all ran down into it, all of them shrieking and yelling and wading into the black water with their hands out, calling her name, their voices crying like lost birds in the dark. Frank closed his eyes. It was over, done. All of them were so much older now, and everything so different. But when he turned from it to look at Willa Moon, he got a jab of pain in the chest so fierce it pushed him back against the bottles and the mirror. Because it wasn't just Kwami and another season of ruined crops and something that had happened a long time ago out by the canal. It was all the miles and miles of unlit land and a neon arrow above the door and a hotel that was falling down and a town that never failed to depend on the wrong crop to save it. It was a one-room apartment above a gas station and a winter of sitting in it watching without hope for something to happen across the street and now a wilted tea rose lying in Shirley's cage. Willa Moon glided around her empty glass as if it had spun her and Frank shut his eyes, unable to bear the view.

"Who said he wanted to dance with Willa Moon?"

He felt something brush his cheek and rest on his wrist. He had a numbness in his mouth that tasted of old pennies. She took his chin and made him open his eyes to look at her.

"Yass?"

She lifted his arm in the air, pressed her fingers into his hand and slid into the crook of his arm. Freddy Romero was singing "*Ya Recuerdo*." Willa Moon led and he followed. From the corner, there was a squeak and the sound of vinyl rubbing skin and Frank groaned and closed his eyes against it. But then he opened them and what he was doing hit him like a slap on the top of his head, wiping out everything he had ever thought, maybe in his whole life.

He was dancing with Willa Moon.

Her heat, her smell, the rustle of her dress when they turned. The black crown of her hair tickled his chin. He bent his wrist back and she leaned into him, one finger curling like a ribbon around the base of his thumb.

The music stopped and changed and stopped. In the quiet that closed in, he heard a thin-pitched squeak and a skitter of footsteps. A moment later the cellar door creaked shut. As simple as that. He groaned and laid his cheek on the top of Willa Moon's head. It was as if he had never been the clumsy and shamefaced Frank Stiles, as if he had been someone else all his life and never known it.

"Don't worry, Willa. She can't touch you. I won't let her. You're a roman candle that never goes out. You are. The rest doesn't matter. Not the swarm, not this bar, not even out there." He inhaled the smell of her and groaned. "Oh God, Willa. Tell me again. Tell me what you said when you said we're not afraid. Because I'm not, Willa. I'm like you. I always was."

"You always was what?" Her voice was blurry. She pulled her head out from under his chin.

Frank closed his eyes. "I love you."

"You?" Her head swayed back as if it was too heavy for her neck. "You don't love me. You don't even know who I am."

Frank shut his eyes. He felt her head thump against his chest, as simple as a woken grumpy child. "All right," she groaned. "Have it your way. Love me if you want."

He led her in an arc, a circle, a criss-cross of grace—but she was holding his sleeve too tightly, as if afraid of falling, wadding it into her fist. He raised his head and spoke to the opposite wall.

"Willa?"

"Then love me goddammitall."

He opened his eyes. "Of course, I do."

"Always."

"Yeah, Willa. Always."

She was crying. He tried to let her go but she yanked him closer and sucked for breath. He shifted so that he could see the two of them in the mirror behind the bar. Her mouth was open, her face twisted against his shirt. When she lifted her eyes and saw him watching in the mirror she pushed him away with a howl.

He had never seen anyone cry so openly, not even Pearl, who cried all the time. He followed her over to a booth and slid into the seat across from her. He held out his hand but she slapped it away. When he told her he understood—a tactic which always defused Pearl—Willa Moon only sobbed harder. She was bawling as if she'd lost her last friend, bawling like a lost child. He was relieved when she finally covered her face.

She laid her head down, cradling it in her arms. Under the blue satin, her whole body was shaking. He watched the top of her head, watched her shoulders heaving. He reached out to touch a strand of her black hair, holding it between two fingers. When she finally stopped, he reached up and turned out the booth light. He felt as if he was very far away, watching her through binoculars.

It took a long time to admit to himself she'd passed out. He needed to take a leak. He stood cautiously to keep the booth from squeaking and stole across the room, out through the kitchen to the back porch.

At the rim of the tar pool darkness the moon was fading, and the sky was beginning to brighten. Frank stood listening. The silence was roaring. Behind him, he heard Billy Quail come into the kitchen and turn on the lights. He was banging pots and pans around and singing to himself in Yiwa because he thought he was alone.

But then Frank realized it was not Billy's singing. It was another sort of sound, a thin, high zithery sound coming from the north. For a moment he wondered if it was only coming from inside his head, but even as he listened, a string of headlights to the west blinked on and then the siren over in Sweetwater began to howl. As if in answer, the singing grew louder. Frank covered his eyes, trying to hold it off a few more minutes, trying to concentrate on the warm, ripening sugar beet smell that was blowing in across the flats; but all he knew was how she'd looked bawling, and the only smell he could remember now was the stale mescal on her breath.

He felt something touch his chest. Thinking it was she, he jerked back, crying out. In the yellow glow from the kitchen light, a large amber-colored grasshopper clung like a brooch to the flap of his breast pocket.

He picked it off and held it in the palm of his hand at eye level. A female by the size of it, too cold yet to fly, rotating its head ninety degrees for a look at his chin. Frank leaned over and put his hand against the porch and the insect stepped to end of his thumb. After a moment, it felt its way off onto the porch. Frank sat down on the steps beside it and leaned back to look up at the sky.

The sky with its stars and its moon that did not care—any more than anything else did—what a man wished or waited or lived out his life for. That was why Willa was right, it *was* better when the waiting was over. All it took was a little leap of faith, and all faith amounted to, in the end, was just whatever there was left to believe. And leaning back to squint up at the sky, Frank believed that these last few stars, still glittering like bottle rocket sparks before the cloud in the east, must certainly be the prettiest he had ever seen. He leaned back and banged on the screen door. The singing was louder, and he could smell the smudgepots being lit. "Hey, Geronimo," he called. "Come on out here." He wanted to tell someone.

---

* Whereabouts unknown when employment census was taken.

(a) Unemployable by present company standards.

(1) Leases land from the Red Spot Land Office Company.

ANGEL, Ester Sykes   Age: 39
    Rte. 286/ Funtown
    Stygo, CO 81103
Position: entertainment worker
Primary Place of Employment: Red Spot Funtown
                                           Carnival
Other income: children employed same
Spouse: deceased
Children: Mick, 21 * (a)
           Ester "Essie," 17
           Mary, 15

BARROWS, Miriam   Age: 41
    1 Bent St.
    Stygo, CO 81103
Position: employee, residence mgr.
Primary Place of Employment: Barrows Red Spot Inn
Other income: main refinery, temp. work
Spouse: Nicholas Barrows, 67 (a)
Children: Harland "Harley," 26

CALLAHAN, August "Augie"   Age: 62
    12 Main Street
    Stygo, CO 81103
Position: retired
Primary Place of Employment: n/a
Other income: R.S. retirement benefits
Spouse: Elsa Callahan, 49
Children: Eliza "Lizzy," 20

FIDDLE, Leeland "Lee"   Age: 27
    Highway 34
    Stygo, CO 81103
Position: road maintenance mgr.
Primary Place of Employment: Stygo & Bent County
Other income: (see William below)
Spouse: Stephanie, 27 ★
Children: Lee Jr., 3 months ★

FIDDLE, William "Billy"   Age: 27
    Highway 34
    Stygo, CO 81103
Position: entertainment worker
Primary Place of Employment: Red Spot Funtown
                                 Carnival
Other income: road maintenance work
Spouse: none
Children: none

HARRISON, John "Fun"   Age: 59
    Rte. 286 / Funtown
    Stygo, CO 81103
Position: entertainment mgr.
Primary Place of Employment: Red Spot Funtown
                                   Carnival
Other income: none
Spouse: Elizabeth Harrison ★
Children: none
Other dependents: Ralph Harrison, 15
                      Paul "Pokey" Harrison, 14

JOPA, Thomas "Pa"   Age: 62
    Jopa K Bar Ranch
    Highway 34
    Stygo, CO 81103
Position: rancher (1)
Primary Place of Employment: Jopa K Bar Ranch
Other income: none
Spouse: deceased
Children: Brice Jopa, 18
          Becca Jopa, 17

LOPER, Jacob "Jake"   Age: 21
    5 Bent St.
    Stygo, CO 81103
Position: refinery worker
Primary Place of Employment: main refinery
Other income: none
Spouse: Eliza "Lizzy" Loper, 20
Children: none

NORMAN, Thomas "Tom Go"   Age: 19
    c/o Sugar Beet Cafe
    2 Main St.
    Stygo, CO 81103
Position: restaurant mgr.
Primary Place of Employment: Sugar Beet Cafe
Other income: Rockeroy Bar, busboy
Spouse: none
Children: none

PESKE, Jewell "Mama Jewell"   Age: 61
    3 Main St.
    Stygo, CO 81103
Position: mgr. of Christians' Residence for the
            Disadvantaged
Primary Place of Employment: 3 Main St.
Other income: none
Spouse: separated (Sy Peske, 65)
Children: none
Adoptees: Christina Roth, 19 (a)
            Hallorie Smith, 10 (a)
            Jane "Baby Annie" Doe, 17

PESKE, Sy   Age: 65
    c/o Peske's Machine Shop or
    Sweetwater Truck Stop
    Stygo, CO 81103
Position: machinist (Retired since the closing of Peske's Red
            Spot Machine Shop); presently works part-time;
            handyman, roustabout, general laborer, etc. (a)
Primary Place of Employment: varies; contact Jack or
                                Frank Stiles
Other income: Red Spot severance pay / occasional
                spouse support
Spouse: separated (Jewell Peske, 61)
Children: none

POTTS, Caroline   Age: 28
    Sugar Beet Cafe
    7 Main St.
    Stygo, CO 81103
Position: cook
Primary Place of Employment: Sugar Beet Cafe
Other income: none
Spouse: none
Children: none

QUAIL, William "Billy"   Age: 68
    Rockeroy Bar
    5 Main St.
    Stygo, CO 81103
Race: N. A. Yiwa Indian
Position: cook
Primary Place of Employment: Rockeroy Bar
Other income: refinery temp. work
Spouse: ★
Children: Quamash "Kwami" Quail(?) (a)

SEYMOUR, Sidney, M.D.   Age: 60
    9 Main Street
    Stygo, CO 81103
Position: physician
Primary Place of Employment: main refinery / residence
Other income: none
Spouse: Sarah Seymour (deceased)
Children: Agatha (deceased)
            Ariel, 31 ★

STILES, Alice "Pearl"   Age: 37
    4 Main St.
    Stygo, CO 81103
Position: food service
Primary Place of Employment: main refinery cafeteria
Other income: Rockeroy Bar
Spouse: none
Children: none

STILES, Frances "Frank"   Age: 35
    4 Main St.
    Stygo, CO 81103
Position: general mgr.
Primary Place of Employment: Rockeroy Bar
Other income: Red Spot Conoco station mgr.
Spouse: none
Children: none

STILES, Jack   Age: 43
    Sweetwater Truck Stop
    Highway 34
    Stygo, CO 81103
Position: truck stop mgr.
Primary Place of Employment: Sweetwater Truck Stop
Other income: none
Spouse: (1)*
Children: Lucille Stiles, 16 *
        Reba Stiles, 17 (a)

WACKETT, John   Age: 49
    Rte. 286 / Funtown
    Stygo, CO 81103
Position: entertainment worker
Primary Place of Employment: Red Spot Funtown
                                 Carnival
Other income: workmen's comp.
Spouse: none
Children: none

WATERS, Samuel "Sam"   Age: 52
   Highway 34
   Stygo, CO 81103
Position: not employed by company
Primary Place of Employment: residence
Other income: corn farming
Spouse: Edith "Edie" Waters, 45 (a)
Children: Ruth Waters, 10

WHATLY, Oren   Age: 34
   2 Bent St.
   Stygo, CO 81103
Position: company law enforcement
Primary Place of Employment: Stygo & surrounding area
Other income: main refinery, temp. work
Spouse: Johanna Whatly, 25
Children: Oren Whatly, Jr., 4
           Tommy Whatly, 2
           Myralise Whatly, 1